THE

Good Fairies

of

NEW YORK

THE

Good Fairies of

NEW YORK

by
Martin Millar

Soft Skull Press
Brooklyn

book design: Dylan Babb
cover design: Edwin Tse

Soft Skull Press
An Imprint of Counterpoint LLC
2117 Fourth Street
Suite D
Berkeley, CA 94710
www.softskull.com
www.counterpointpress.com

Distributed by Publishers Group West

Library of Congress Cataloging-in-Publication Data

Millar, Martin.
  The good fairies of New York / by Martin Millar.
     p. cm.
  ISBN-13: 978-1-933368-36-8 (alk. paper)
  ISBN-10: 1-933368-36-5 (alk. paper)
  I. Title.

PR6063.I34G66 2006
823'.914--dc22

2006019074

Printed in the United States of America

10 9

"My main concern in life," said Kerry, "is collecting my flower alphabet. This is a difficult task, as some of the flowers involved are rare and obscure, particularly in New York. Once I have my flower alphabet, however, all sorts of good things will follow.

"For one thing, it will look beautiful. For another, it may well benefit me with regard to the strange wasting disease I suffer from, because an Ancient Celtic flower alphabet is bound to be very powerful. Also it will be a devastating weapon against Cal, a man who, by going back on his promise to teach me every New York Dolls guitar solo, proved himself to be one of the lowest forms of life. Once my flower alphabet wins the East Fourth Street Community Arts Association Prize, his life will be in ruins."

The nurse smiled at Kerry, placed a thermometer gently in her mouth, and busied herself with the preparations for the operation.

AN INTRODUCTION

I owned this book for well over five years before I dared to read it.

It was not that I dislike Martin Millar's books. Quite the reverse—I've been a fan of his work for almost twenty years. I fell for his prose, wry and honest and gentle and smart, the day I picked up *Milk, Sulphate and Alby Starvation*. I fell for his characters: I like an author who likes his own characters, and Mr Millar's characters always seemed like people that he had very much enjoyed spending time with. I enjoyed his plots, which have that enjoyable sense of rightness that good stories ought to have—you don't feel, reading it, that someone made this up, you feel instead that someone found out what happened and wrote it all down for you.

I bought this book several years after it came out, because I had moved to America where they never quite got the hang of publishing Martin Millar novels. And then, once I had obtained it, it sat on my shelf for five years, unread, a book that I knew would be funny, smart, contain great and likeable characters and have a plot that would feel like a proper satisfying story.

Five years . . .

It was all in the title.

Authors are odd animals. For those five years I was gearing up to write, and then I was writing, a novel called *American Gods*, all about what happened when the gods and the fairies and the creatures of legend came from the Old World to the New. So, while I owned *The Good Fairies of New York*, I did not dare to read it. It was,

I saw from the back cover, about Scottish fairies who came to New York. I didn't need to read any more. I was troubled enough already. For me, probably for any author, the biggest worry is that someone will write the book that I'm writing, and write it first. Or, at any rate, that someone's going to write a book that looks like a book that I'm hoping to write. If they do that, and they do, then I'm not allowed to read their book until after I've written my book. This is mostly because, if they have written my book, I'll give up on the spot and be very sad. It's also because I don't want to have to worry about copying the other books, and the best way to do that is simply not to read them.

I was writing—or at least, in the beginning, thinking about writing—a book called *American Gods*, in which all the things in which people have ever believed had come to America: gods and fairies and dreams; and now somebody—someone whose work I liked, at that—had written a book in which fairies came to New York. I was, I feared, screwed. So I bought the book, put it on the shelf, and only years later, when my book was safely out of my head and onto the paper, did I dare to start to pick up *The Good Fairies of New York*.

I was relieved to discover that it covered very different territory to my book, but mostly I was happy I was finally reading it, and wishing I'd read it before.

Millar writes like Kurt Vonnegut might have written, if he'd been born fifty years later in a different country and hung around with entirely the wrong sort of people. He makes jokes with a straight face, and never follows the jokes with a nudge to the ribs or a rim-shot on the cymbal, instead he gets on with telling the story, funny and moving and wise and filled with people you care about, even if some of them are very small and others have personal habits that, frankly, leave a great deal to be desired.

Millar started off good, and with his own unmistakable voice, writing books like *Milk, Sulphate and Alby Starvation* (a book I was once amused to find mis-shelved under *Medicine: Nutrition*), *Ruby and the Stone Age Diet* and *Lux the Poet*. He was good and then he got better.

The Good Fairies of New York is a story that starts when Morag and Heather, two eighteen-inch fairies with swords and green kilts and badly-dyed hair fly through the window of the worst violin-ist in New York, an overweight and antisocial type named Dinnie, and vomit on his carpet. Who they are, and how they came to New York, and what this has to do with the lovely Kerry, who lives across the street, and who has Crohn's Disease and is making a flower alphabet, and what this has to do with the other fairies (of all nationalities) of New York, not to mention the poor repressed fairies of Britain, is the subject of this book. It has a war in it, and a most unusual production of Shakespeare's "A Midsummer Night's Dream" and Johnny Thunders' New York Dolls guitar solos. What more could anyone desire from a book?

When I first read it, I assumed that I would not have to wait long before The Good Fairies of New York became a Broadway Musical, or even a Movie, like Shrek for grown-ups. This has not yet happened, due, I am forced to conclude, to the lack of imagi-nation of Broadway producers and the reluctance of Hollywood people to spend hundreds of millions of dollars on Morag and Heather, on Dinnie and Kerry. I do not understand this reluctance at all; nor do I understand why Martin Millar isn't as celebrated as Kurt Vonnegut, as rich as Terry Pratchett, as famous as Douglas Adams. But the world is filled with mysteries.

This is a book for every fiddler who has realised, half-way through playing an ancient Scottish air, that the Ramones "I Wanna Be Sedated" is what folk music is really all about, and gone straight into it. It's a book for every girl with home-dyed hair and fairy wings who can't honestly remember what happened last night. It's a book for people of whatever shape and size who like reading good books.

I owned it for more than five years before reading it, then lent my copy to someone I thought should read it, and never got it back. Do not make either of my mistakes. Read it now, and then make your friends buy their own copies. You'll thank me one day.

Neil Gaiman,
October 2004
64 Miles from New York

THE

Good Fairies

of

NEW YORK

ONE

Dinnie, an overweight enemy of humanity, was the worst violinist in New York, but was practicing gamely when two cute little fairies stumbled through his fourth-floor window and vomited on the carpet.

"Sorry," said one.

"Don't worry," said the other. "Fairy vomit is no doubt sweet-smelling to humans."

By this time, however, Dinnie was halfway down the stairs, and still accelerating.

"Two fairies just came through my window and were sick on the carpet!" he screamed on reaching Fourth Street, not fully realizing the effect that this would have on the passers-by till the men sweating with sacks round a garbage truck stopped to laugh at him.

"What'd you say?"

"Upstairs," gasped Dinnie. "Two fairies, with kilts and violins and little swords . . . green kilts . . ."

The men stared at him. Dinnie's monologue ground to a halt.

"Hey," called the foreman, "leave that dumb homo alone and get back to work. C'mon, let's get busy!"

"No, really," protested Dinnie, but his audience was gone. Dinnie stared hopelessly after them.

They didn't believe me, he thought. No wonder. I don't believe myself.

On the corner, four Puerto Ricans kicked a tennis ball back and forth. They looked pityingly at Dinnie. Chastened by the public ridicule, Dinnie slunk back into the old theater on the ground floor of his building. His room was right at the top, four flights up, but Dinnie was unsure whether he wanted to climb them or not.

"I like my privacy," he grumbled. "And my sanity."

He decided to buy some beer from the deli across the street.

"But if I find two fairies in my room when I get back, there's going to be trouble."

Five more fairies, all suffering from massive confusion due to beer, whisky and magic mushrooms, were at that moment fleeing in drunken terror from the chaos of Park Avenue to the comparative shelter of Central Park.

"What part of Cornwall is this?" wailed Padraig, narrowly escaping the wheels of a honey-roasted peanut vendor's trailer.

"The Goddess only knows," replied Brannoc, and tried to help Tulip, who had become entangled in the dangling reins of a sightseer's horse and trap.

"I think I'm still hallucinating," whimpered Padraig as a tidal wave of joggers trundled down the path towards him. He was saved by Maeve, who hurried them on, deep into the undergrowth.

They flopped down to rest on a quiet patch of land.

"Are we safe?"

Noise still surrounded them, but no people were in sight. This was a relief. They were invisible to most humans, but so many hurrying feet were a terrible danger.

"I think so," replied Brannoc, oldest fairy present and something of a leader. "But I'm beginning to suspect we're not in Cornwall anymore."

A squirrel hopped over to join them.

"Hello," said Brannoc politely, despite his terrible hangover.

"What the hell are you?" demanded the squirrel.

"We are fairies," answered Brannoc, and the squirrel fell on the grass laughing, because the New York squirrels are cynical creatures and do not believe in fairies.

Meanwhile, back on Fourth Street, Dinnie swallowed a mouthful of Mexican beer, scratched his plump chin and strode confidently into his room, convinced that he had imagined the whole thing.

Two fairies were sleeping peacefully on his bed. Dinnie was immediately depressed. He knew that he did not have enough money to see a therapist.

TWO

Across the street, Kerry was just waking up in her soft bed of old cushions. Kerry, as well as being wondrously lovely, could pick up some tattered old piece of material and make it into a beautiful cushion, or maybe a hat or waistcoat, with ease.

She was also a talented painter, sculptor, singer and writer, a dedicated shoplifter and a serious collector of flowers. And she was a keen guitarist, but her technique was dreadful.

Most people loved her, but despite this, she was not happy this morning. Her unhappiness stemmed from four main sources. The first was a news report on television about terrible floods in Bangladesh, with pictures of bodies, which upset her badly, and the second was the chronic wasting disease she was suffering from. The third was her lack of skill on the guitar. Despite hours of practicing, she still could not play Johnny Thunders' guitar solo from "Pirate Love."

The fourth, far outweighing these at the moment, was her complete inability to make up her mind as to what looked best pinned in her hair: carnations or roses. Kerry's hair was based loosely on a painting by Botticelli and the right flowers were essential.

She sat gloomily in front of the mirror, trying first one then the other, reflecting bitterly that it was no use at all dyeing your hair to a beautiful silvery blue when you still had problems like this to face up to.

The flower alphabet was coming on well and she now had fifteen out of the thirty-three flowers she required.

Across the street the fairies were waking up.

"Where are our friends?" muttered Heather, brushing her golden hair away from her beautiful eyes.

Dinnie stared balefully at her.

"I don't know what you are," he said, "and I don't care. But whatever you are, get the hell out of my room and leave me alone."

Dinnie MacKintosh was not noted for his politeness. He was not really noted for anything except his rudeness, intolerance and large appetite.

"My name is Heather. I am a thistle fairy. And this is Morag. Could I have a glass of water, please?"

"No!" thundered Dinnie. "You can't. Get out of here!"

"What sort of way is that to speak to us?" demanded Heather, propping herself up on a tiny elbow. "Where we come from, anyone would be honored to bring us a glass of water. They'd talk about it for years if we so much as appeared to them. We only appeared to you because we heard you playing a Scottish violin tune."

"Extremely badly," interjected Morag, wakening slightly.

"Yes," agreed Heather, "extremely badly. The violin had an interesting tone, but frankly it was the worst rendition of the 'Reel of Tulloch' I have ever heard, and that is saying something. It was worse than the playing of the blacksmith's son back home in the village of Cruickshank, and I wouldn't have thought that was possible."

"My playing is not that bad," protested Dinnie.

"Oh, it is. Really terrible."

"Well no one invited you here to listen to it," said Dinnie angrily.

"But don't worry," continued Morag, fingering her tiny violin. "We will show you how to do it properly. We are good fairies, and always happy to help. Now kindly bring us some water."

"Hi," purred a naked woman on the TV, rubbing her breasts with a phone. "We're the cream team and we give ass, head and pussy so well it's a fucking crime. Call us at 970 T-W-A-T."

"I must still be hallucinating," said Morag. "I swear I will never touch another magic mushroom. Except possibly for medicinal purposes."

Dinnie strode up to the bed and loudly requested that Heather and Morag leave immediately as he did not believe in fairies. The fairies burst out laughing.

"You are funny," chortled Heather, but the action of laughing upset her precarious hangover and she threw up again, all over Dinnie's arm.

"Well, he certainly believes in us now!" screamed Morag.

"Don't worry," said Heather. "Fairy vomit is no doubt sweet-smelling to humans."

They both went back to sleep and no amount of abuse from Dinnie could wake them.

THREE

The homeless clustered everywhere in New York. Every street corner had its own beggar with dull eyes who asked passers-by for change with little hope of a response. Every park was laced and ribboned with makeshift plastic tents and stinking blankets rolled up as sleeping bags. These homeless had the most hopeless of lives. No government scheme would ever give them a fresh start. No charity would ever be rich enough to house them. No employer would ever give them work without their having a place to live, or at least some clean clothes, and clean clothes were never going to appear to anyone who sweated all day in a swelteringly hot park. All they could do was get by the best they could until they died, and this did not happen nearly quickly enough as far as the decent citizens of New York were concerned.

One homeless old man sat down for a rest on Fourth Street, sighed, closed his eyes, and died.

"Another one dead," muttered Magenta, arriving on the scene. Magenta herself was a homeless beggar, though a fairly young one.

"At this rate I'll have no troops left."

She saluted the fallen warrior and toiled her way along to Broadway, keeping a wary eye out for Persian cavalry divisions. Even though she was still some way from the army of

Antaxerxes and was not expecting trouble, she knew that being this deep inside enemy territory she had to be careful.

Back in England, in Cornwall, Tala the King was most upset at the flight of Petal and Tulip. As his children and rightful heirs they were already being whispered of by rebels as suitable replacements for himself.

"Find them," he instructed Magris, his Chief Technician, "and bring them back."

Of course, the Fairy King of Cornwall could not know that at this moment two of the fugitives were waking in an empty room on Fourth Street.

They immediately began to argue.

"I feel terrible."

"Well, it's your own fault," said Morag. "The way you were throwing back mushrooms and whisky."

"What do you mean? You were the one who vomited over your new kilt."

"I did not. It was you. You can't take your drink. Just like the well-known saying, never trust a MacKintosh with a glass of whisky or a fiddle."

"That's not a well-known saying."

"It is in my clan."

"Morag MacPherson, you will be the death of me. And if you insult the MacKintoshes' fiddle playing one more time, I will be the death of you."

"There is no fiddle playing to insult."

They glared at each other.

"What happened to the others?"

"I don't know. We lost them after you fell unconscious and I had to help you."

"I did not fall unconscious, you did. No MacPherson fairy can hold her whisky."

"Any MacPherson can hold it better than a MacKintosh."

The argument intensified until it became too much for their hangovers. Heather swore an obscure Scottish oath and stumbled off the bed, rubbing her temples. She approached the window. The wings of a thistle fairy are only useful for short flights at the best of times and now, weakened by mushrooms, whisky, beer and jet-lag, Heather had a hard time fluttering up to the window-sill.

She finally made it and looked down on East Fourth Street. She gasped. To a Scottish thistle fairy, used only to hills, glens and the quiet village of Cruickshank, it was an amazing sight. Cars and people everywhere, children, dogs, noise and at least ten shops within twenty yards. In Cruickshank, there was only one shop, and very few cars.

"What is this place? Where are we?"

Morag joined her. Her first sober sight of their new environment made her forget the argument and she clutched Heather's hand.

"I think it must be a city."

"What's a city?"

"Like a big town. Like lots of villages put together. I think we must be in Glasgow."

"But we were in Cornwall," protested Morag. "Cornwall isn't close to Glasgow, is it?"

Heather shook her head. She did not think so, but her geography was as shaky as Morag's. Since leaving Scotland neither of them had had much of an idea of where they were most of the time.

They peered down at the street where a ragged man with a shopping bag tramped forcefully along the sidewalk, spilling small children out of the way.

This ragged man was Joshua. He was in pursuit of Magenta who had made off with his recipe for Fitzroy cocktail, a drink consist-

ing of shoe polish, methylated spirits, fruit juice and a secret con-
coction of herbs.

After pursuing her down First Avenue, he had lost sight of her
when she dodged down the subway. She was a cunning adversary
but he would never give up the hunt for his recipe, the most precious thing he had ever had in his possession.

"What happened to our friends? Where are Brannoc and Maeve
and Padraig and Petal and Tulip?"

It was impossible to say. They could be anywhere in this city.
Neither of them could remember much except waking up in a
huge bumpy machine and being tossed into the street in a beer
crate. Their friends had presumably been carried off by the
machine. They started to argue again about whose fault it was.

"Right you two," said Dinnie, stomping back into the room.
"Get out of here immediately and don't come back."

"What is the matter with you?" demanded Heather, shaking
her golden hair. "Humans are supposed to be pleased, delighted
and honored when they meet a fairy. They jump about going, 'A
fairy, a fairy!' and laugh with pleasure. They don't demand they
get out of their room immediately and don't come back."

"Well, welcome to New York," snarled Dinnie. "Now beat it."

"Fine," said Heather. "We'll go. But don't come crying to us if
your lineage is cursed to the seventh generation."

"Or even the thirteenth."

They stared at each other. A cockroach peered out from behind
the cooker, then went about its business.

Morag, generally the more rational of the two fairies, tried to
calm the situation.

"Allow me to introduce myself. I am Morag MacPherson, thistle fairy, from Scotland."

"And I am Heather MacKintosh, thistle fairy. And greatest fiddler in Scotland."

"What?" protested Morag. "I am the greatest fiddler in Scotland."

Heather fell about laughing.

"How dare you laugh at my fiddle playing. I am Morag MacPherson, champion of champions," continued the dark-haired fairy.

"Well I'm Dinnie MacKintosh and you two can just beat it."

Now Morag burst out laughing.

"What's so funny?"

"He's a MacKintosh," chortled Morag. "No wonder his fiddle-playing is so bad. The MacKintoshes never could carry a tune."

Heather looked uncomfortable.

"He's only a beginner," she said, but Morag continued to laugh uncontrollably. She was greatly amused at this turn of events. In her eyes she had won the argument.

"How dare you laugh at a fellow MacKintosh," raged Heather, who could not bear to see her clan belittled in any way. "Even a human MacKintosh is worth more than a lying, cheating MacPherson."

"How dare you call the MacPhersons lying and cheating," screamed Morag.

The fairies' green eyes blazed.

"Look—" said Dinnie, but he was ignored.

"You are lying and cheating. Lying, cheating, thieving, no good—"

"Heather MacKintosh, I hope I never see you again!" shouted Morag, and hopped out the window.

There was a silence.

Heather looked glum. Shouts drifted up from the soccer play-ers on the corner below.

"Call 970 C-L-I-T for the hottest phone sex in New York," whispered a naked woman on the television screen.

"I'm lost in a strange city and now my friend's gone away and it's all the fault of your stupid violin playing," said Heather, and began to cry.

FOUR

"Yes," admitted Kerry, tucking a pair of gloves underneath her waistcoat. "I do shoplift compulsively."

"Why is this," enquired Morag. "Is it kleptomania, which I once read about in a human newspaper?"

"No, it just burns me up the way there are nice things everywhere and I can't afford to buy them."

"Are you poor?"

Kerry was.

"And often depressed. But I have been much more cheerful since you appeared." Outside in the street, Kerry tried on her new gloves with satisfaction.

The fairy, after arguing with Heather, had flown across the street and there had the good fortune to meet Kerry, one of the very few humans in New York who could see fairies.

Anyone who knew Kerry, with her long silvery blue hair, her hippie clothing, her flower alphabet and her quixotic quest to play New York Dolls guitar solos, would not have been surprised to learn she could see fairies. They would only have been surprised that she had never seen one before.

She had made friends with Morag immediately and now they regularly went shoplifting together. Kerry fed Morag, found her whisky and listened to her fiddle-playing and her stories. She also explained the intricacies of her flower alphabet and the reasons why she loved the New York Dolls and why she was determined to be revenged on Cal, a faithless and treacherous lead guitarist who rehearsed with his band across the street in the old theater.

"My revenge on Cal will be terrible and complete," she told the fairy. "He will bitterly regret ever promising to teach me all the guitar solos on the first New York Dolls album, then letting me down so disgracefully. Particularly as I fucked some dreadful, boring roadie merely so he would give me a guitar."

"Excellent," agreed Morag. "Give him hell."

Kerry had several methods of revenge in mind, but mainly she planned to defeat his entry for the East Fourth Street Community Arts Association Prize.

"They are producing a version of *A Midsummer Night's Dream* at the theater," she explained. "Cal is directing it. They imagine that they will win this year's prize. But they won't. I will. My radical new version of the ancient Celtic flower alphabet, assembled afresh for the first time in centuries, will win the prize. And this is good, because I am very fond of flowers. I used to take flowers to bed with me, when I was little."

"So did I," said Morag.

On Fourth Street, a beggar asked for money.

"I'm sorry, I don't have any," said Kerry. "But have this instead."

"What was that?" asked Morag.

"A postcard of Botticelli's *Venus and Mars*," Kerry told her. "A most beautiful picture."

Morag was unclear as to how this would help a starving beggar, but Kerry said it would do him a world of good.

"If more people had nice pictures by Botticelli there would be much less trouble everywhere. I base the flower arrangements in my hair on *Primavera*, the world's greatest painting."

"Now let me get this straight," said Spiro, chief squirrel of Central Park who, alerted by reports from his subordinates, was paying the strange new creatures a visit.

"You call yourselves fairies. You are invisible to almost all humans. You come from a place called Cornwall. You lived happily there until some technically minded fairy called Magris invented the steam engine and precipitated an industrial revolution in your fairy society. Consequently Tala, your king, started moving previously well-contented fairies out of the fields and gardens and into workhouses, thereby producing a miserable and oppressed fairy kingdom almost overnight, complete with security police and travel permits. Am I right so far?"

Brannoc and the other fairies nodded.

"Whereupon you, being mainly concerned with playing music and eating mushrooms and having no interest in working twelve hours a day in a factory, decamped for Ireland, aided by two Irish fairies. On the way you met two Scottish fairies who claimed first to have been run out of their home town for playing Ramones songs on their fiddles, and second to have been run out of Scotland for some other offense they would not admit, and then you found a field of magic mushrooms and ate them all. Instead of carrying on fleeing."

"We were tired."

"Right. Subsequently you drank more whisky and beer than you can remember, then you got bundled onto a truck somehow and next thing you know you were being driven up Fifth Avenue, after presumably being loaded onto some sort of cargo-carrying airplane. Is that it?"

The fairies nodded miserably. Central Park was better than the furious streets beyond, but it was not like home.

"Well, cheer up," said Spiro. "It's not too bad. At least you ended up in America. You can speak the language, more or less. You can rest here a while, and what's to stop you sneaking out to JFK and boarding a plane home?"

"We can't go back. Tala the King wants us dead."

"Looks like you're stuck here then. But what's so bad about that? New York is a good place, you'll like it."

Somewhere around City Hall Magenta halted for lunch, unwrapping a half-eaten pizza she had picked up on a bench along the way. She ate it warily.

She was sure that Tissaphernes was in the area. Tissaphernes was head of the Persian cavalry. Magenta's force consisted mainly of Hoplites and Pelasts, so she had to be careful not to be outmaneuvered. She rose and carried on up Broadway.

Outside, the sun shone. Inside, Kerry and Morag got drunk. This was not good for Kerry as her wasting disease left her short of energy, but it made her mind feel better.

"Two in two days," she mused, referring to another tramp who had lain down and died on the sidewalk outside. Kerry and Morag placed some flowers around the corpse and called an ambulance. Tired now, she lay down to rest and asked Morag the reason for her continuing argument with Heather.

"It is partly because I am a MacPherson and she is a MacKintosh," explained Morag. "And there is a very ancient and bitter feud between the MacPhersons and the MacKintoshes. I will tell you all about this later. But even apart from that, Heather showed herself to be of dubious character right from the start.

"It was way back when we were children, or bairns as we might say in Scotland. Both our mothers had taken us, along with our clans, to a great fairy piping and fiddling contest. The gathering was held near Tomnahurich Hill, which is close to a town called Inverness.

"My mother told me that the gathering used to be held on the hill itself back in the old days, when the Fairy Queen lived right inside it, but now humans have built a cemetery there. Thomas the Rhymer is buried there. He was a famous Scottish prophet and fairy friend, sometime in the tenth century. Or eleventh or twelfth. Or some time, I forget. Anyway, with a cemetery there, we couldn't use the hill anymore. There are many places we can't go anymore because of humans. But we still like the area. It is beautiful, and convenient for all the fairy clans to come and play.

"I remember on the way there we passed by Culloden. There are many stories about Culloden but they are all very painful for the Scots, so I will not tell them just now. Anyway, the festival was a wonderful event. All the great pipers and fiddlers were there, and singers and jugglers and acrobats and storytellers and horse-racers and everything you could imagine, everyone bright and happy and colorful."

Morag smiled at the memory.

"I was very excited because my mother had entered me for the junior fiddle competition. It was the first time I would ever have played in front of anyone else but my own clan. I had been practicing all year. I was going to play 'Tullochgorum.' That is the tune I was playing outside your window a while ago. I don't wish to be immodest, but these days I am famous throughout Scottish fairydom for my playing of 'Tullochgorum.' It is a famous strathspey, which is a kind of Scottish reel, but it is very difficult to play well. A Scottish fiddler can build a reputation just by the way she performs it. Rabbie Burns, who is the best poet in the world, called it the Queen of Songs."

She laughed.

"My mother wanted me to play something less difficult but I was a very determined bairn, if rather quiet. And in fact, though all the great fiddlers were there, playing in competitions during the day and for fun all night, and I heard the tune played by some of them, I did not really think that any of them did it better than me.

"Well, come the day of the junior contest, I was a bundle of nerves. My mother, who despite many faults did understand the fiddle, poured a dram of whisky down my throat and told me to get on with it. The whisky calmed me down and when I heard the other young competitors I realized that I was a better fiddler than any of them. It was my turn next and I was just starting to feel confident when a pale, sickly-looking little fairy with unusual golden hair got up and played. She played 'Tullochgorum,' and it was the best version anyone had heard at that festival. The audience went wild. Naturally I was furious."

"Naturally," agreed Kerry. "It was a mean trick."

"It certainly was. And I might have been put off except I could see from the blonde fairy's kilt that she was a MacKintosh and I certainly was not going to let a MacKintosh fairy get the better of me. I had the pride of my clan to think of. Also, my mother would have been mad as hell.

"So I stepped up, closed my eyes and played. And was I good?"

"Were you?"

"I was sensational. The best version of 'Tullochgorum' heard this century, according to independent witnesses."

"So did you win?"

"No, it was a draw between me and Heather. She got the sympathy vote because she was such a sickly-looking child. Also it was rumored that the MacKintoshes had bribed the jury. But I wouldn't have minded being first equal except—and I know you will find this hard to believe—Heather and her mother started complaining that Heather's rendition had obviously been superior and suggested the MacPhersons had bribed the jury on my behalf! Can you imagine?"

"So what happened?"

"I attacked Heather and tried to kill her. Unfortunately she was tougher than she looked and we had a terrible fight. We both had cuts and bruises and missing teeth before we were pulled apart. And then after that we made friends."

"Just like that?"

"Yes. After all, we were the best two fiddlers there. And when the wise fairy woman was bandaging us up, we started to like each other better. That's how me and Heather met. And also how we got our excellent fiddles. They were our prizes. But she will never admit that my version of 'Tullochgorum' was better than hers."

"And this underlying tension makes you argue?"

Morag was not sure what 'underlying tension' meant, but agreed that that was probably it.

"Also, she claims it was her idea to form a radical Celtic band, but it was mine. I heard the Ramones first. The blacksmith's son had their first three records."

Morag mused.

"And now I have ended up in New York, where they come from. This is obviously fate, as one reason Heather and I left Cruickshank in the first place was because all the other fairies ganged up on us for playing garage-punk versions of Scottish reels and wearing ripped kilts. They didn't like us dyeing our hair, either."

She picked up her fiddle, played a majestically traditional version of 'Tullochgorum,' then got down to the business of working out the notes of the guitar solo on the New York Dolls' 'Bad Girl.' Once she had it worked out she could try to show Kerry how to play it, although as Morag was not a guitarist and Kerry had little musical knowledge, this was proving to be an arduous business.

"That miserable motherfucker Cal could play this solo," grumbled Kerry, eyes shining with hatred.

Across the street Dinnie looked out of his window.

"That's funny," he muttered. "I'm sure I heard someone playing the violin over there."

"Ignore it," said Heather. "It was just some cat in heat. Now, are you sure you don't have a wee drop of whisky anywhere?"

FIVE

After Morag's departure, Heather stayed with Dinnie. Dinnie was enormously unenthusiastic about this.

"Go live somewhere else," he told her.

Heather replied that she could not desert a fellow MacKintosh in trouble.

"I'm not in trouble."

"Yes you are."

In reality, Heather had nowhere else to go. But as it seemed like an obvious stroke of fate that that the first person she had met in this metropolis was a fellow MacKintosh, she was content to stay. With her ability to make herself invisible, Dinnie was powerless to chase her out, much as he would have liked to.

She sat now eating his cookies and working his TV remote control. Only dimly familiar with the small choice of programs available back in Britain, she was fascinated by the fifty channels that beamed and cabled their way to Dinnie's TV.

Dinnie was out, trying to earn some money. He had snarled at Heather that he was behind with his rent and was in danger of being evicted.

"Fine, fine," said Heather, unaware of what this meant.

He had spent a miserable morning hanging around the courier office waiting for work. As a bicycle courier, Dinnie was a disaster. Too fat to ride quickly enough and too argumenta-tive to accept less than good work, he was lucky to earn any-thing at all, and served mainly as a figure of ridicule for the other riders.

Today, like all other days, had proved unrewarding and Dinnie rode home in a foul temper, wondering where he was to find money for his rent.

Turning onto East Fourth he cycled past Kerry. Dinnie frowned his deepest frown. He saw Kerry often, and he detest-ed her.

"You cheap tart," he would mutter to himself as she waltzed by.

"You faggot guitarist," he would hiss quietly after whatev-er lithe and attractive young man was trooping along beside her.

"You slut," he would mumble, when peering out of his win-dow at four one lonely morning to see Kerry offloaded by a cab driver and helped, drunk and giggling, up the steps and into her apartment.

Dinnie was deeply attracted to Kerry.

Heather greeted him brightly as he appeared.

"Don't speak to me," he grunted. "I've decided not to believe in you in the hope you'll disappear."

"Why are you so rude to me?"

"Because I am a sensible human being and I have no time for nasty little fairies."

Dinnie opened a can of corned-beef hash, heated it in a fry-ing pan, ate it and piled the dishes into the sink. He was fastid-iously untidy. In his two large rooms there was nothing clean or in its proper place. He had an unusually large living space for the rent he paid, as the rooms he occupied above the theater were not meant to be lived in. He rented them illegally from the caretaker. Because of this he lived in constant fear of eviction, even when he was not behind with his rent.

"I saw an amazing show," said Heather, "about a big family who owns oil wells in Texas. Would you believe that one of them had a car crash and couldn't breathe because of his injuries, so his secretary, who had trained as a medical student, jabbed a knife into his throat, stuck a pen into his windpipe and blew into it until an ambulance arrived, thus saving his life? An emergency tracheotomy, I think they called it. When he held her hand in the ambulance and told her he loved her I was moved to tears."

Ignoring her, Dinnie picked up his violin and left, bicycling determinedly up Second Avenue.

"Where are we going?" said a disembodied voice from the handlebars.

Dinnie wailed and fell off the bike.

"I'm not surprised you don't make any money as a courier," said Heather, brushing the dirt off her kilt. "You keep crashing."

Dinnie coughed and spluttered.

"Do you need a tracheotomy?" asked Heather hopefully, unsheathing her tiny sword.

"What the hell are you doing here?"

"I wanted an outing."

Dinnie was going busking, something he only did in times of dire need.

He chained his bike at St. Mark's Place. Three separate ragged and homeless young men begged dimes from him, but he ignored them and began to play.

Heather shook her head in disbelief. Dinnie's playing was bad beyond description. Passerby crossed the street to avoid him, and shouted insults. The small-time coke dealer on the corner left for his lunch break. The ragged homeless people, who had suffered too much to be driven away by a violin, just turned the other way.

After half an hour of painful wailing Dinnie had earned nothing whatsoever. He sadly unchained his bike and made to leave.

Heather was appalled to see a MacKintosh musician so defeated.

"Don't go," she whispered.

"What's the point of staying?"

"Play again," instructed Heather, and she leapt onto Dinnie's violin, deadening the strings. Unseen by the rest of the world, she played her fiddle while Dinnie mimed. She played her way through some thrilling Scottish reels—"The Salamanca," "Miss Campbell of Monzie," "Torry Burn" and various others, each linked with some of her favorite Ramones riffs—before plunging into a stirring version of "Tullochgorum."

The crowd burst into loud applause. Coins rained into Dinnie's fiddle case. Dinnie scooped them up and made a triumphant exit. He was so pleased with the money and the applause that he was moved to say thank you to Heather, and all in all it would have been a memorable occasion had he not found that his bike had been stolen.

"You stupid fairy," he raged. "Why did you make me play after I'd unchained my bike?"

"Well I didn't know it would be stolen," protested Heather. "Bikes don't get stolen in Cruickshank."

"Damn Cruickshank!" shouted Dinnie and stormed off.

Magenta cycled serenely down First Avenue. Joshua, some way behind, shook his fist in frustration. He had almost caught her when Magenta, showing great tactical skill, had leapt onto an unchained bicycle and made off.

Unable to run far, Joshua soon abandoned the chase and flopped down on the sidewalk.

He started to shake. Without regular doses of his Fitzroy cocktail he got withdrawal symptoms, but his mind was so addled by it he could not remember the recipe without the piece of paper Magenta had stolen.

A homeless acquaintance of his ambled by and offered him a drink of wine, which helped, though only a little.

"Damn that Magenta," snarled Joshua. "And her stupid classical fantasies."

"I always knew it was a mistake to take her drinking in the library," said his friend. "Who does she think she is now?"

"Some ancient Greek general," grumbled Joshua.

"It's not my fault you live in a city populated by thieves and criminals," said Heather, fluttering after Dinnie. "I earned money for you, didn't I?"

"Twenty-three dollars. Where am I going to get a bike for twenty-three dollars?"

"At a bike shop," suggested Heather, but this seemed to enrage Dinnie even more.

When an old woman with three worn and filthy coats haning off her shoulders asked him for some change he swore at her quite violently.

Back at the theater he stepped over a body at the foot of the stairs without so much as a glance. Heather did stop to look. It was another dead tramp. Too far gone for a tracheotomy.

It is just awful the way these people die on the street here, she thought. Why is there no one to look after them?

Downstairs at the theater, rehearsals for Cal's production of *A Midsummer Night's Dream* were underway. When Dinnie heard the actors' booming voices, he would scream abuse through the floorboards. He was not a fan of Shakespeare.

"Never speak to me again," said Dinnie to Heather, who thought he was being most ungrateful.

She was used to ingratitude, however. After she and Morag had spent countless hours in Scotland developing their new fiddle techniques, dyeing their hair and experimenting with inhaling the vapors of fairy glue, neither of their clans had been very pleased. Both their mothers had in fact threatened them with expulsion from their clans if they did not stop trying to subvert the youth of the Scottish fairydom. When they later enquired politely of Callum MacHardie, famous fairy instrument maker, whether he could make them an electric amplifier, he had actually reported them to their Clan Chiefs, thereby subjecting them to long lectures on what was and was not suitable behavior for fairies.

"Tripping around in meadows is fine," their chiefs had told them. "And helping lost human children home again. Also, increasing the milk supply of friendly farmers' cows. But a large-scale youth rebellion is quite out of the question. So go home and behave yourselves."

Right after hearing this Heather and Morag had fluttered around the valley wearing hand-painted T-shirts saying 'First Mohican Fairy on the Block,' but as no one else knew what a block was, the joke fell flat.

Morag stole what small pieces of food she could carry, loose cookies and bagels, and fed them to the homeless. She had not appreciated it before in her village, but here she could see that being human could involve some very unpleasant things. Despite this she was still marveling at the wonders of New York.

Kerry was twenty-five and had lived in New York since she was fifteen, so she did not marvel anymore, but she liked it.

They sat in a bar in Houston Street, drinking beer from a bottle. The fairy enthused about some South American musicians they had seen busking in Broadway.

"What good players they were. And lovely rhythms."

"Mmmm," replied Kerry.

"And weren't those two boys romantic, sitting kissing on

the fire escape?"

Morag was keen on the fire escapes that snaked down the fronts of buildings and she frequently hopped up and down them, looking in the windows.

"Mmmm," said Kerry.

"I am sure I am having a better time with you than Heather is with that lump of a MacKintosh. I can tell that he is much too mean to give Botticelli postcards to beggars, or flowers."

Kerry was silent.

A cheerful young barman gathered up the bottles from their table, giving Kerry a hopeful grin. Kerry stared into space.

"It is nice the way people smile at you all the time, Kerry."

A tear trickled down Kerry's face.

"Let's go home," she said.

They walked home, noticing as they did a worried-looking bag lady slinking her way up Third Street, taking cover behind cars and lamp-posts.

"Another madwoman. There are a lot of them here."

Magenta was not exactly mad, but after plunging over the handlebars of the bicycle due to too much alcohol, she was not feeling very well. She retired to a doorway, fished out her stolen copy of Xenophon's *Expedition to Persia* and thumbed through it for a hangover cure.

The birds and animals gossiped in Central Park.

"I've heard from a blackbird," said a pigeon to a squirrel, "who heard from a seagull, that the albatrosses are looking for some creatures who sound a lot like these fairies."

The pigeons and squirrels looked at the fairies and wondered if there was going to be trouble.

"I miss Heather and Morag," said Brannoc.

"Well I don't," answered Padraig, tuning his fiddle. "I never met such argumentative fairies in my life. I'm not surprised they were run out of Scotland. If they ever made it to Ireland, they'd be run out of there as well."

Violin tuned, Padraig started to play. He played "The Miltdown Jig" slowly, then a little faster, then broke into a dazzling version of "Jenny's Welcome to Charley," a long and complicated reel. Maeve joined in on her pipes. Fairy musicians have magical control over the volume of their instruments and the two blended perfectly.

The animals stopped gossiping to watch and listen. Maeve and Padraig were the best fairy musicians in Ireland, and this is almost the same as saying they were the best musicians in the world, although Heather and Morag might well have had something to say about that.

Kerry's apartment consisted of two small rooms. The bed was raised on a platform and underneath she stored her clothes. She lay on the bed. Morag sat beside her.

"Back in Scotland," said the fairy, "I am well known for my astute psychic insights. And it strikes me that since I have been here you have never really been happy. Am I right?"

Kerry burst into tears.

"I was unhappy long before you arrived," she said.

"Why? Your life seems good. Braw even. Everyone likes you. You have lovers queuing up at your door, though you turn them all away."

Kerry stared at her poster of the New York Dolls. They stared back at her, pouting.

"I turn them away because of my disease," explained Kerry.

Kerry had Crohn's disease, a most unpleasant ailment which rots away the intestines.

"After a while doctors have to cut out the diseased parts."

Morag shuddered. This was beyond her imagination.

Kerry undid her shirt. On her left side she had a bag taped

to her skin.

The meaning and function of a colostomy bag were not obvious to Morag until Kerry explained.

Morag stared gloomily out the window. Life streamed past but she was not entertained. She was imagining what it would be like to have a hole cut in your side for your excreta to empty into a bag.

The sun was particularly strong today. The heat was over-powering. Pedestrians sweated their way along the sidewalks and drivers cursed and sounded their horns.

Kerry patted her triple-bloomed Welsh poppy, an almost unimaginably rare flower and pride of her collection. Finding it growing wild in a ruined building was what had set her off on her quest for the flower alphabet. She kissed it, stroked it and spoke to it nicely.

Next she checked her new *Mimulus cardinalus*, a pretty red and yellow flower, the newest addition to her alphabet. The cut flower hung upside-down to dry. Once it was dry she would spray it with hairspray to preserve it and add it to the other fifteen preserved blooms covering her floor.

Cal had stopped going out with her when he learned about her colostomy, saying that he could not see himself having a relationship with someone whose excreta emptied into a bag at her side. This made Kerry feel very bad.

Morag sighed. Being human did seem to involve some very unpleasant things.

SIX

"I don't want a violin lesson," declared Dinnie. "And I don't want you here. Go and join your friend."

"She isn't my friend," protested Heather. "Just someone I had the misfortune to meet. I took pity on her. To tell you the truth, she annoyed the hell out of me."

Heather settled down with a thimbleful of whisky, skillfully removed from the bar on the corner.

"Brag, brag, brag, all the time. Just because she's got a few psychic powers. So what? Psychic powers are ten-a-penny among fairies. Common as muck. I wouldn't take them as a gift. Of course, her basic problem is that she's insanely jealous of my spectacular golden hair which made all the male fairies in Scotland fancy me like nobody's business. Drove her crazy. Gentlemen prefer blondes, as we used to say in the Highlands."

"You both dye your hair," Dinnie pointed out, eyeing the crimson ends of Heather's blonde tresses with disapproval.

"But mine always looked better," chuckled Heather. "Morag's is too dark to dye properly."

Dinnie stared glumly at the wall. If he had believed in fairies, he wouldn't have expected them to spend all their time bitching about each other's hairstyles.

He eyed his violin. A defeated expression settled on his large pink face. It was too difficult for him. He would not make any progress. He did not even genuinely like the instrument anymore, although when he had first seen it in the junk shop, lying under a pile of broken trumpets, it had seemed to mean something to him.

At school he had learned to play for a short while before giving up. He had bought the violin and music book because they reminded him of school, which was the last time he had had any friends.

"Pick it up," instructed Heather.

"No."

This was all very frustrating to Heather. If Dinnie did not learn the fiddle she would lose face in front of Morag. Heather had unwisely boasted to her that with her superior fiddling skills it would be no trouble to teach Dinnie to play.

Now she realized that Morag had trapped her into this rash statement by deliberately laughing at the MacKintoshes.

"When you can play well you'll earn money busking."

"Not soon enough to prevent me getting evicted," grunted Dinnie. After the theft of his bike, busking was a sore subject.

Heather ran her fingers through her golden hair, admired herself in the mirror, and thought desperately. She would die before admitting failure in front of Morag MacPherson.

"Well, how about this," she suggested. "I will try and teach you the fiddle. If you make progress, you will be pleased. If you fail to make progress, I promise to go away and leave you in peace. Then you will also be pleased."

The notion of Heather disappearing into the depths of Manhattan was indeed pleasing to Dinnie.

"Okay," he agreed, "teach me something."

"I'll make you lick my snatch, you filthy worm," snarled a woman's voice. "Call 970 D-O-M-M now!"

"Please turn off channel twenty-three," said Heather. "It is not conducive to fiddle teaching."

Dinnie laughed.

"I might have known you fairies would be prudes."

"I am not a prude. In the Highlands I was widely regarded as the hottest lover since the great fairy piper Mavis MacKintosh, who once lay with eighteen men, twelve women and the chief of the MacAuly fairies in one night, leaving all of them pleased but exhausted. I just don't like phone domination. Kindly turn it off."

In Central Park, Brannoc was moodily eyeing Petal and Tulip who were holding hands under a bush. As they were brother and sister they had every right to hold hands, but it made Brannoc jealous. Brannoc had been infatuated with Petal since the day he arrived in Cornwall, a wandering minstrel from the cold, unknown shires of northern England.

Maeve and Padraig were asking the squirrels where they might find a drop of Guinness.

"In many bars," one of the squirrels told them. "This place is full of Irish people who love to drink Guinness and their bars have shamrocks outside them. But it would mean going onto the streets which are full of humans. And though you claim that back in Ireland any human would have been delighted to stop whatever they were doing and bring you some beer, here I am not so sure."

Maeve declared that she would go right that minute and find some because she was Maeve O'Brien from Galway and not afraid of humans or anything else, but Padraig was cautious and said they should wait.

Petal and Tulip were lost in a dream. They frequently disappeared into the trance-like fairy dream state to forget about their father. They were the children of Tala the King and they knew he would never stop pursuing them.

"Wow," said Spiro when he learned of this "You're the King's children. Imagine! Royalty! Right here in Central Park!"

But Maeve poured scorn on this because she detested

English royalty. She dismissed Petal and Tulip's arguments with their father as standard English aristocratic stupidity.

"Never did a day's work in their lives," she muttered, and played a fierce jig on her pipes.

Brannoc strummed his mandolin lightly. He was teaching Petal and her brother mandolin and flute. When they were not dreaming, they were quick to learn.

Dinnie was not quick to learn.

"Use the bow delicately. You are not trying to saw the fiddle in half."

Heather, five minutes into her first lesson, was beginning to regret it. So was Dinnie. He stood up, tall, fat and awkward.

"I've changed my mind," he said. "I'll learn some other time."

Heather clenched her teeth.

"Dinnie, you are trying my patience. A fairy teaching you music is a big honor. Enjoy it."

"Big fucking honor, you dumb elf," rasped Dinnie.

"Eat shit, you fat sonofabitch," rasped Heather. She had already picked up a few useful expressions in the bar on the corner.

They glared at each other.

"Pick up the fiddle."

"I've got other things to do."

"Like what? What do you have planned for this evening? Visiting a few friends, perhaps?"

Dinnie narrowed his pudgy eyes uncomfortably.

"You don't have any friends, do you?"

"So what?"

"So this: despite your incredible rudeness to me, really you are pleased to have me around because otherwise you would have no one at all to talk to. In this enormous city you do not have so much as one friend. Is this not true?"

Dinnie picked up the remote control and switched on the TV. Heather nimbly leapt onto the control and switched it off.

"Do not feel bad about it, Dinnie. I have been busy learning about this place. Apparently loneliness is not uncommon. I know this because I read an article about it in a young women's magazine that an old man was reading in the bar. In Cruickshank, everyone is friendly with everyone else. How it is that with so many people here some people aren't friendly with anyone at all is beyond me, but I can fix it for you."

"Don't bother," grunted Dinnie.

"It is no bother. Among Scottish fairies I am famous for my ability to win friends. Of course, with my golden hair and otherworldly beauty, everyone generally wanted to make friends with me anyway—something, incidentally, that used to drive Morag crazy—but even so, I could always win over the unfriendliest troll or Red Cap."

"Fine. If you meet any trolls down Fourth Street, you won't have any problems."

"I am the best fiddle player in the world. And you will soon be good as well, with a MacKintosh fairy helping you. You should have heard Neil Gow before my mother showed him a few tricks."

"Who is Neil Gow?"

"Who is Neil Gow? He was the most famous Scottish fiddler ever. He was born in Inver, which is close to where I come from. He is buried in the churchyard of Little Dunkleld, a very pretty place, although we fairies are not too keen on churchyards as a rule. I could tell you many interesting stories about Neil Gow."

"And no doubt you will."

"Later. Anyway, his technique was appalling till my mother took him in hand. My family taught all the best Scottish violinists, and I'm sure I can teach you. So stop eyeing the TV control and let's go.

"Lesson one. 'The Bridge of Balater,' a slow strathspey, but stirring in the hands of a master."

Heather played "The Bridge of Balater." It was a slow strathspey, but stirring in her hands. Each Scottish Snap snapped in a way rarely heard since the time of Neil Gow. On the windowsill, birds settled down to listen. Outside on the street, Rachel, an old bag lady, hearing Heather's beautiful playing, rested her weak legs on the theater steps.

"I'm glad I heard something worthwhile before I die," she murmured to herself, and warmed her insides on the good fairy's aura.

Upstairs, Heather beamed at Dinnie.

"Now you try."

Dinnie, his battered copy of *The Gow Collection of Scottish Dance Music* balanced uncomfortably on his knee, struggled his way through "The Bridge of Balater." The birds departed and Rachel was jerked unwillingly back to the land of the living.

"Appalling," said Heather, truthfully. "But you will be better in no time. Now look. This symbol on the music means a turn, played like this . . . And that symbol means tremolo, played like this . . . Try it."

Dinnie tried. He still produced a horrible noise. Heather sighed. She had far less patience as a teacher than she imagined.

"Dinnie, I can see that desperate measures are called for. And you had better believe that this is a rare honor, granted to you only because you are a MacKintosh in trouble. Also because my ears won't stand much more. Hold out your hand."

She touched his fingers. Dinnie felt them go slightly warm.

"Now try again."

Dinnie looked at his warm fingers, and tried again. For the first time ever, he managed to produce a sound which was tolerably close to being musical.

Aelric squatted under a bush. It was deepest night, and all of Cornwall was quiet. His five followers sat behind him, tense and ready. At Aelric's sign, they fluttered into the air, flew over the shed containing the spinning looms, magicked fire into their hands and set it alight.

The shed burned brightly, but before the alarm was even raised Aelric and his followers had fled safely away into the night.

Aelric was the leader of the Cornish Fairy Resistance Movement, and the one ray of hope for the fairies under their oppressive leaders. However, as his resistance movement consisted of just him and five others, and Tala was by far the most powerful ruler the kingdom had ever seen, his task seemed a hopeless one.

Still, the burning of the weaving shed was a useful piece of economic sabotage. Aelric had learned about economic sabotage from a book on terrorist tactics he had found in a human library, and so far it seemed to be working well.

Dinnie made some progress, but soon complained of sore fingers.

"Play it again," instructed Heather.

"My fingers are sore."

"Haud your wheesht, you fat lump," cried the fairy eventually.

"Don't try your obscure Scottish expressions on me," said Dinnie. "And I would rather be a fat lump than an eighteen-inch freak in a tacky kilt."

"How dare you. And after me actually teaching you a tune."

"I would have learned it anyway."

Heather was outraged.

"You have the natural talent of a haggis," she said, and

departed into the night.

A very few people, like Kerry, are born with a natural ability to see fairies. Others, like Magenta, develop the ability through drinking strange potions like meths, boot polish and fruit juice.

"I take it you are an otherworldly servant of Tissaphernes, Persian satrap of the region?" said Magenta.

"No, I am Heather, a Scottish thistle fairy."

Magenta was not convinced and gripped her sword.

"Well I am Xenophon. I am leading the Greek mercenaries in aid of Cyrus, brother of King Antaxerxes, against that same Antaxerxes. And if you are a servant of his, tell him the end is nigh."

A car with speakers built into the back trundled past, vibrating the area with its music.

I'd like to play my fiddle through a system like that, thought Heather, which made her think of her and Morag's plans for their band. This made her sad.

Magenta marched off, firmly and happily fixed in her fantasy.

SEVEN

"Everyone's yellow," said Morag. "We're in Chinatown," Kerry told her.

They were taking their daily walk. While in Chinatown, Kerry was on the lookout for a flower of the Gingko Biloba, a Chinese tree.

"How did the flower from a Chinese tree end up in the ancient Celtic alphabet?" Morag enquired.

Kerry did not know. She supposed the Celts were well-traveled.

"Or else it used to grow in other places. Anyway, it is one of the rarities that make my flower alphabet difficult to collect."

Morag scanned the horizon for Gingko Bilobas. She had supposed, on first hearing of the project, that a flower alphabet meant one flower beginning with A, another with B, another with C and so on, but apparently it was more complicated than that. The flowers required corresponded to ancient Celtic symbols, rather than modern English letters, and not only did they have to be the right species, but the right color as well.

No Gingko Bilobas being in sight, Morag studied the people.

"What a place this New York is. Black people, brown people, white people, yellow people and people sort of in-between. I love it."

"So do I," said Kerry. "But sometimes the people fight."

"Why?"

"Because they are different colors."

Morag had a good laugh.

"Humans are so dumb. If fairies were all different colors, they wouldn't fight about it."

Today Kerry had woken up cheerful, and even dealing with her colostomy bag had not depressed her. Morag knew that it would later, however, and was still grappling with the problem of what to do about it. Being a fairy she had some magical healing powers, but these did not extend to complicated surgical matters.

A small brooch in the form of an eight-sided mirror caught Kerry's eye and she walked into the shop to look at it. It was an unusual shop, a second-hand place full of clothes and jewelry, with a few books and cards on the counter. Behind the counter were some old instruments. Morag examined them while Kerry asked the Chinese owner about the brooch. It was not for sale.

"Why not?" said Morag, outside.

Kerry shrugged.

"I don't know. He just said it wasn't for sale."

They carried on along the street and Kerry took the brooch from her pocket.

"You are an excellent shoplifter," said Morag, admiringly. "I didn't notice a thing."

Morag spotted some lobsters in a large tank at the front of a restaurant.

"Why are those lobsters living in that shop?" she asked.

"They stay in that tank till a customer wants to eat them. Then they get cooked."

"What?!"

Morag was appalled. Back in Scotland, while wandering round the east coast, she had had many pleasant conversations with lobsters. She had no idea that people ate them. When they went home later for Kerry to eat and take part of the daily dosage of steroids that controlled her Crohn's disease, Morag felt rather depressed about it.

She unwrapped her violin from its green cloth and placed it gently under her chin.

"That is a lovely tune," said Kerry.

"Thank you. It is a well-known Scottish lament. Although to tell you the truth I am a little bored with this sort of thing. If Heather hadn't been such an ignorant little besom and got us thrown out of Scotland in disgrace, our radical Celtic thrash band would have been rousing the nation at this very moment."

The sight and sound of Morag gloomily toying with a mournful lament made Kerry sad as well and by the time twilight came they both agreed that the only thing to do was go to bed depressed with the phone muffled by a pillow.

Kerry said goodnight to her flowers, kissed the fabulous Welsh poppy and lay down to sleep.

Downstairs in the theater across the road Cal was auditioning young actresses for the part of Titania in *A Midsummer Night's Dream*.

Heather looked on with some annoyance.

"None of them was anything like a fairy queen," she complained later to Dinnie, but Dinnie was too busy smearing extra peanut butter on his chocolate cookies to take much notice.

"I followed a bag lady yesterday," continued Heather. "She was under the illusion that she was Xenophon, an Athenian mercenary in the year 401 BC, going to fight for Cyrus, the pretender to the Persian throne, against his brother Antaxerxes."

"I hate the way you make up these stupid stories," said Dinnie. "Leave me in peace."

Unable to sleep, Morag rose and determined to free the lobsters.

"Poor little things."

She hopped on a car heading downtown, feeling adventurous.

"Rather like James MacPherson," she muttered. James MacPherson was a famous robber and fiddler in seventeenth-century Scotland and a good friend to the fairies, before he was hanged.

On the next street a firecracker went off, and a few folks were out on the sidewalk, but it was mainly quiet.

She found the restaurant and waved a cheery hello to the lobsters. Setting them free was not difficult. Most locks are no trouble for a fairy to pick and soon she had them swimming to safety down the sewers.

A spectacular success! thought Morag. A triumph in fact. A smooth operation, entirely without hitch. MacPherson the Robber himself could not have done better.

"And what exactly do you think you're doing robbing a restaurant on our patch?" demanded a voice behind her. Morag whirled round, and found to her great surprise that there was a very angry-looking fairy with yellow skin glowering at her.

Morag fled.

On the Corner of Canal Street she hopped on a passing motorcycle which raced away much faster than she could fly and she hung on for dear life. Behind her an angry horde of Chinese fairies waved their fists at her and looked for vehicles to mount to pursue her.

"White devil," they screamed. "Raiding our restaurants."

As the motorbike neared Fourth Street Morag risked injury with a spectacular leap onto the ground, then ran for home. A quick glance over her shoulder showed no one in pursuit. She prayed that she had shaken them off. Fortunately for her the motorcyclist had been drunk and had driven like a madman.

Aha! thought Magenta, creeping up Broadway and seeing

the Chinese fairies in unsuccessful pursuit of Morag. Early skirmishes. Antaxerxes has sent out his captain Tissaphernes and a
host of oriental soldiers. She realized that battle was near and,
to steady her nerves, had a good pull at the bottle of Fitzroy
cocktail. The boot polish stained her lips a grim purple color
but she was much heartened.

Thinking that she should take cover she headed for East
Fourth Street and ducked into the theater.

Inside, Cal was giving instructions to the actor playing
Theseus, Duke of Athens.

"You're a duke. Be regal."

"Preposterous," announced Magenta, appearing in the
wings. "Theseus was never Duke of Athens."

"What?"

"Theseus was never Duke of Athens. The rank of duke was
unknown in Athens for one thing."

"Well, how the hell do you know," demanded Cal.

Magenta drew herself up. Magenta had not been weakened
by her life on the streets. Thirty-five years old and muscular,
with short-cropped iron-grey hair, she could be an intimidating
sight when roused.

"'How do I know?' I was born there."

"Beat it, bag lady," said the performer.

Magenta dealt him a dismissive blow on the ear.

"I resign," said the actor, from the floor. "Serious performers cannot work in these conditions."

Morag sped into Kerry's room, safe home. Kerry had woken up
and was sitting on a cushion making a hat to match her light
blue hair, drinking beer and listening to the radio.

"Devilish yellow fairies—" began Morag, but Kerry interrupted her.

"Morag, I was just thinking about you. Listen to the news."

The newscaster was describing the day's events in Brooklyn, where there had been serious trouble between Koreans and Dominicans after a fight in a deli. The incident had developed into a major disturbance, and the deli was now surrounded by pickets.

"Another race row," said Kerry. "What a pity humans cannot be like fairies, as you mentioned this morning."

"Right," said Morag, looking at the ceiling.

Kerry switched off the radio and looked thoughtful.

"What does 'devilish yellow fairies' mean?"

"Nothing. Nothing at all. Just a pleasant Scots blessing. We often say it on meeting an old friend."

Morag hunted out her whisky supply and made for bed.

"I think I'll go to sleep now. If anyone calls, tell them I'm not in."

"Do you have to sit on my shoulder?" complained Dinnie.

"Why not? It's a good fat shoulder. Lots of room."

"My shoulder is not fat."

"Yes, it is."

They stopped on the corner to argue. This heated discussion between a violinist and an invisible fairy would have drawn attention in some places. On a corner of East Fourth Street, no one took any notice.

They walked on, Dinnie more grumpy than usual but Heather completely unaffected by the argument. Dinnie was on his way to the supermarket on Second Avenue where he could shop cheaply and buy his favorite cookies.

"Any change?" asked a beggar. Dinnie ignored her. Dinnie's meanness saddened Heather. She did not think it was fitting for a MacKintosh to refuse to help the poor.

"She doesn't have a home. It is terrible not to have a home."

"I couldn't care less. If you're so bothered about it, go and build her one. It'll get you out of my hair."

"I've never been in your hair. It's too dirty."

Dinnie had thick black hair, bushy and uncombed. Along with his height, this sometimes gave him a wild man look, particularly when he had not shaved – either because he could not be bothered or because he could not get the hot water to work.

He did not appreciate personal criticism from a fairy and endeavored to walk on in silence. This was not possible with Heather on his shoulder.

"Why does the steam rise from the pavement?"

"I've no idea. And they're called sidewalks."

"Really? Are we there yet?"

"No."

"Fine. I'll tell you a story while we're traveling. I'll tell the sad tale of why I was expelled from the lovely lochs and glens of Scotland. Why I can never go back to see the beautiful heather-covered hills and the snow-tipped peaks of Glencoe. How I am forever denied the pleasure of heather ale and whisky, as expertly brewed and distilled by the MacKintosh fairies, and will never again see the bonnie wee churchyard of Inver."

Dinnie gritted his teeth. "Get on with it."

"I was just setting the atmosphere. Anyway, one night, dark, stormy and lashing with rain, Morag and I were traveling in Skye, which is an island off the west coast of Scotland. We were on our way to the great MacLeod fairy fiddling competition. Conditions were terrible, but being a MacKintosh I was not too bothered. Morag, however, was whining and complaining even more than usual about being wet and cold. The MacPhersons never did have any true mettle. She was about to lie down somewhere and give up when I took matters in hand and found us a castle to shelter in."

"You found a castle? Just like that?"

"Castles are not uncommon in Scotland. In fact, Scotland is full of castles. We found a room that was nice and dry. There wasn't any sign of a bed but there was a comfy-looking casket on the floor so we climbed in. There was nothing inside it except a large piece of green cloth."

A cab crawled past, blaring its horn at the truck in front, which was blaring its horn at the car in front of it, which was temporarily stalled by another car which had stalled. The vehicles behind the cab joined in, sounding their horns in a huge impatient chorus, although there was nothing any of the drivers could do except for wait. Dinnie threaded his way across the street.

"Morag was still complaining about being cold of course, so to shut her up I got out my sword and cut a few pieces of this material for some blankets. And very good blankets they were too. We had an excellent sleep. But guess what the cloth turned out to be?"

"I don't care."

"It was the famous MacLeod fairy banner!"

Heather waited for a gasp of astonishment from Dinnie. None came.

"Aren't you amazed?"

"No."

"Haven't you heard of the famous MacLeod fairy banner?"

"No."

Heather was surprised. She assumed that everyone had heard of it.

"It is one of the most famous fairy artifacts in Scotland, as famous and important to the Scottish fairies as the MacPherson Fiddle and the MacKintosh sword.

"It was given to the human MacLeod clan by the fairies some time in the eleventh century and they keep it in their ancestral home, Dunvegan Castle. It saved the clan and must only be unfurled in an emergency. You can't play around with the MacLeod fairy banner. No one is meant to even touch it. Cutting it up for blankets is absolutely out of the question.

"Anyway, next day, ignorant of what we'd done, we went

on our way. We used the blankets to wrap our fiddles in, thinking that they might come in useful later. But when we reached
the site of the competition and unwrapped our fiddles, there
was uproar. The MacLeod fairies were going to kill us there and
then for mutilating the banner. I told them it was an accident
and I hadn't even realized we were in Dunvegan Castle, let
alone that I was cutting up the Fairy Banner, but they seemed
to think we'd done it deliberately. MacLeod fairies are noted for
their low intelligence. Unfortunately there are an awful lot of
them and we had to flee back to the mainland on a porpoise.

"And after that they wouldn't let up. They chased us everywhere. Even the fact that we are good fairies and are known for
never committing malicious deeds didn't make any difference.
Hence Morag's and my flight from Scotland. Now we can
never go back and it's all because that dumb bitch Morag kept
complaining about the cold. She has ruined my life."

"Well," said Dinnie, sensing an opportunity to discomfort
Heather. "It was you who cut up the banner."

"Only to help a weaker creature. And I wasn't to know it
was the famous MacLeod Banner. What did they leave it lying
around in a casket for?"

Dinnie was tired by this time. The walk from Fourth Street
to the supermarket had made him pant and he concentrated on
shopping quickly and returning home.

"You might at least express some sympathy," said Heather,
as he loaded up with cookies and cans of corned-beef hash.

"Why? I don't care about you being chased out of
Scotland."

"But it is a terrible thing to be homeless."

"Bah!"

Dinnie had a brief argument with the woman at the check-
out when he mistakenly thought she had overcharged him,
then headed home.

"Just the man I was looking for," said the caretaker, meeting Dinnie on the steps. "I'm evicting you."

Dinnie stamped his way up to his rooms and flung his shopping bag on the floor.

"I am sorry," said Heather. "It is a terrible thing—"

"Don't say it," snarled Dinnie, and savagely opened a can of corned-beef hash.

The albatross landed heavily on the shore of Cornwall. Magris was there to greet her. He was the King's Chief Wizard, although he now liked to be known as Chief Technician, and his wings were neatly folded under a long grey cloak.

"Have you any news for me?"

The albatross shook her head.

"There is no sign of them in any of the kingdoms we fly over, We have seen wars, famines and plagues, ships, trains and cars, ants, camels and lizards, Spriggans, Church Grims and Merwomen, but we have not seen your two fairies or their friends.

Magris frowned. He was annoyed, but he knew better than to criticize the albatrosses.

"Please continue your search."

The bird nodded and flew off. Albatrosses are not given to idle chatter, as a rule. Neither was Magris. He was too furious about the rebel Aelric and his economic sabotage. Warehouses and factories were burning all over the kingdom.

It was being whispered by the rebels that if Petal and Tulip were to rule instead of Tala, things would be well in the kingdom.

Petal and Tulip were resting in a peaceful little clearing surrounded by the thick undergrowth of Central Park, listening to Maeve and Padraig play their tin whistles. They played "Ballydesmond" and "Maggie in the Woods," and Petal and Tulip tapped their feet to the cheerful polka rhythm.

"And when will we see Doolin again, I wonder?!" said

Maeve. Doolin in Ireland was famous for its tin whistles and
the two fairies had spent much time there, listening and playing. They thought for a little while about the good times they
had had in County Clare.

Magenta had never been keen on the twentieth century. When
her father died, electrocuted by his word processor after washing his hands and not drying them properly, she had gone off it
entirely. She was not too keen on washing either.

The Xenophon fantasy she sank into was a pleasant escape
and a good way of keeping her spirits up while hiding from
Joshua. She and Joshua had been lovers once, before Magenta
caught him with another bag lady and stole his cocktail recipe
in retaliation, knowing that he could not live without it.

Now, however, prowling along the sidewalk, she considered giving it up. The fierce alcoholic potion was wearing off
and she was blearily aware that she actually bore little resem-
blance to the legendary Greek hero.

A fairy shape flickered in the distance.

"Must still be hallucinating."

Heather was looking sadly at another corpse, another old
tramp who had died of illness, exhaustion and hopelessness.
That made three in three days. She hated the way these people
just expired on the streets and stayed there. People would walk
right past and not even look. This would never have happened
in Cruickshank.

A fairy will put a flower in a corpse as a sign of respect, and
Heather went to look for one. Inside the theater, next to Cal's
guitar, she found a glorious poppy with red, yellow and orange
blooms, and scooped it up to lay on the corpse.

She played a sad lament, then departed.

Magenta reached the corpse and was appalled to see that it
was someone she knew well, a woman Magenta had begged

with and been friends with for fifteen years.

She sat down gloomily and took a long drink from her Fitzroy cocktail. The city seemed like an unpleasant place to be.

"To hell with this," muttered Magenta's subconscious. She rose to her feet majestically.

"Cyrus is dead," she announced to the waiting troops. "My dear friend and benefactor, killed in battle. Now how will we Greeks ever find our way home across thousands of miles of hostile territory?"

She picked up the flower that Heather had left and marched away purposefully.

The albatross made a heave landing on the Cornish beach.

"We have found them," she told Magris.

"Where?"

"One of them was spotted by a sparrow in New York, talking to an old woman."

"Thank you," said Magris, and gave the albatross a golden reward.

EIGHT

The loss of Kerry's triple-headed Welsh poppy was a mind-numbing blow.

Kerry stared at the space where it should have been, trembling with shock and fury. Morag, perched on top of a speaker and listening to Suicide, flew over to ask her what was the matter.

"My poppy is gone."

In Kerry's book of Celtic myths the Welsh poppy was the centerpiece of the mystic alphabet. Furthermore, it had to be one with three blooms and this was so rare as to be practically unobtainable.

"I found it after the police bulldozed a crack factory," wailed Kerry. "There isn't another one in America!"

How it could have vanished was a mystery.

Cal buzzed the apartment. When he came up he brightly thanked Kerry for the loan of her flower.

"My Titania was panicked by a strange bag lady who attacked the theater. I had to get her something to calm her down. I let myself in with your key and took a flower. I knew you wouldn't mind. I'm afraid someone took it though. Wasn't important, was it?"

The Chinese fairies were not at all happy that a restaurant in their area had been robbed by an interloper, but this was nothing compared to their horror on discovering that their Bhat Gwa mirror was missing. A Bhat Gwa mirror is specially designed to reflect bad Feng Shui, which means various forms of misfortune, and was most precious to the Chinese fairies. This mirror, a small octagon, had been left in the shop of their human friend, Hwui-Yin.

Without it to reflect away misfortune all sorts of calamities would occur, particularly as it was nearing the time of the Festival of Hungry Ghosts, when dissatisfied spirits roamed the earth.

They sniffed around the shop, scenting out clues as to where it had gone.

"The strange white fairy with multicolored hair has been here," they cried, picking up Morag's aura, as fairies can do. They assumed that she had stolen it—a reasonable assumption, although really it had been Kerry, and the mirror was now pinned to one of her Indian waistcoats as a pleasant decoration.

"That was a braw punch," said Morag. "Reminded me of the time I had to fight off the MacDougal clan single-handedly."

"Thank you," said Kerry, nursing her bruised hand.

"Do you think Cal's nose was actually broken? He ran away so quickly I couldn't see."

Kerry said she hoped it was, and muttered about the further dire revenge she would now take. She was deeply depressed by the loss of her flower, and presumed that it was deliberate sabotage by Cal.

Right now she was busy untaping her colostomy bag before disposing of it. She hated the noises it sometimes made.

Morag perched on her shoulder.

"How will we replace the flower?"

"It can't be replaced."

"Nonsense," replied Morag. "Am I not here to help you? I will scour the city."

Kerry took her sterilized saline preparation and a swab to clean the hole in her side. Morag flitted down onto a pile of Velvet Underground bootlegs, peering briefly at a photo of a young and sad Nico.

"Would you like me to steal you some cocaine from the dealer on the next block? It might give you inspiration."

Kerry laughed.

"How do you know that?"

"Another psychic insight."

Kerry did not think stealing cocaine for her was a very good idea. She carefully taped a ring of cardboard onto her side for today's bag to fit on.

"Well, how can I cheer you up," asked Morag, slightly frustrated. She never had these problems cheering up the unhappy women in Cruickshank.

"Tell me a story."

Morag was pleased.

"What an excellent idea. I will tell you the story of the feud between the MacPhersons and the MacKintoshes, a tale which will enlighten you about the glories of Scottish culture and also help you understand how Heather turned out to be the total bitch she is today."

And she settled down comfortably on the Velvet Underground bootlegs to do just that.

"From around the twelfth century, there was a powerful confederation of clans in Scotland, the Clan Chattan. This was made up of the MacPhersons, with whom my tribe of fairies is associated, the MacGillivrays, the MacBeans and the Davidsons. And the accursed MacKintoshes—"

"Please don't spit on the floor again," said Kerry.

"Very well. Anyway, the MacPhersons were the natural

leaders of this federation. For one thing they were braver and smarter than anyone else. They were also stronger and more beautiful than anyone else. And their pipers were the finest in the land, naturally enough, as my family was around to teach them, and we are famous pipers as well as fiddlers.

"In addition to this, the MacPhersons were descended from Muireach, the Parson of Kingussie in 1173, and he was the father of Gillechattan Mor, who was the undisputed leader of the Chattans, and of Ewan Mor, who started the MacPherson line. So the MacPhersons were descended from the man who started the Chattan line, and were their natural leaders. But when leadership of the Chattans passed to Eva, daughter of Dougall Dall, in 1291, Angus, Sixth Laird of the accursed MacKintoshes, kidnapped her, forced her to marry him and stole the leadership."

Kerry was meanwhile taping on a clean plastic bag to collect the excreta which would today ooze out of her side.

"Of course, the MacPhersons never accepted this but down through the centuries the MacKintoshes used every dirty trick and subterfuge imaginable to hang on to their ill-gotten position. Nothing was too base for them. They cheated, connived, sold out to the French, English or anyone else who would pay them, and generally disgraced the good name of the clans by their shocking behavior. I believe they are still doing it.

"So you see," concluded Morag now flushed with emotion, "with a background like that it was inevitable that Heather would turn out bad. Thieving, cheating and ratting on her former lover comes naturally to her. It's in her blood."

"Oh, come on," protested Kerry. "Surely she can't be that bad?"

The small fairy snorted derisively.

"Ha! Never a day went past in Cruickshank without Heather committing some disgraceful act. If the farmer's milk went missing, they sent out search parties for Heather. If a villager's cottage burned down, 'Where's Heather?' was the cry.

Honestly, it's a wonder she wasn't lynched from the hawthorn bush long before she was drummed out of the country. I tell you, she may be a thistle fairy but she is the most miserable, cheating, unscrupulous scunner—"

"Oh dear," said Kerry kindly. "You are desperately in love with her, aren't you?"

"Certainly not. All she ever did was brag that she could dye her hair brighter than mine. That was before you introduced me to the art of pre-color bleaching, of course. If I never see her again, it will be fine with me. She has ruined my life. It was her stupid idea to cut up the MacLeod Fairy Banner for blankets. I was perfectly comfortable without a blanket. Now I'm exiled from Scotland all because of her. And even before that she had her mother on to me, accusing me of being a bad influence because she learned to play the whole of the first Anthrax album on her fiddle. The suffering she has caused me is appalling."

Kerry, having finished the process of changing the colostomy bag, was now dressing. Because of the bag's location on her body, she could not wear anything which was tight around the waist, and the colorful leggings which she had tried to put on proved to be too constricting. She gave a deep sigh and hunted for something looser. Morag studied her while she dressed.

"On the other hand," said the fairy, "compared to some things, I have not really had a lot of suffering."

Kerry took a small bottle from the shelf for the dose of steroids that would prevent the disease from flaring up.

"Maybe not," she said. "But your story is sad. Let's go and buy an enormous pizza and wallow in it. Then we will try and think of a way to replace the poppy. I will win the East Fourth Street Community Arts Prize or die in the attempt."

NINE

Dinnie tried to persuade the caretaker not to evict him but the caretaker was adamant. He was risking his job by letting anyone rent the top-floor rooms as it was illegal, and if Dinnie could not pay, he had to go.

"But I am the only respectable presence here. Without me the entire building will be taken over by faggots. I am a good tenant, quiet, no trouble to anyone. I'll have the money tomorrow."

The caretaker wavered. Unfortunately Heather at that moment succumbed to an irresistible urge to perch invisibly on his shoulder and play a series of fast jigs.

"Leave tomorrow," said the caretaker, and departed.

"What the hell did you do that for?" screamed Dinnie. The fairy could offer no reasonable explanation. The outraged Dinnie threw both of his sandals at her and she departed in a huff.

Dinnie slumped in front of his TV.

"I should have swatted her with the fiddle," he muttered.

Under Heather's tuition, Dinnie had learned to play "The Bridge of Alar" and "The Miller o' Drone," another well-known Scottish strathspey. His practicing had become more enthusiastic. He could still not play well, by human standards, and by fairy standards he was quite abominable, but it was definite

progress. Dinnie had almost been moved to show some grati-
tude to Heather, but had restrained himself.

"Make a thousand-dollar pledge to God now," said a handsome TV evangelist. "Break your cycle of poverty and misfortune. Pledge me a thousand dollars now and your troubles will
melt away with the help of the Lord."

Dinnie swore out loud at the evangelist and switched over.

"We're here waiting for your call," said a naked woman
soothingly, rubbing her body with a red telephone. "Nice, pink,
warm, young, juicy pussy, on 970 C-U-N-T."

"What are you watching?" said Heather, hopping in the
window with a satisfied whisky grin on her face.

"None of your damn business."

"What does nice, pink, warm, young, juicy pussy mean?"

"How dare you show your face back here."

"Do not worry," said Heather. "I have forgiven you for
throwing your sandals at me."

On the outskirts of Heaven there was great activity. Bodies
went to and fro, talking excitedly to one another and looking
earthwards.

"What's happening?" said Johnny to his friend Billy.

"Coming up to the Festival of Hungry Ghosts," Billy told
him. Billy had died some years before Johnny and knew more
of what went on here. "All the Chinese spirits with things on
their minds, maybe some affair that didn't go too well or some
other unfinished business, get the chance to go down and look
around, maybe fininsh a few things off."

"Well, that is interesting," murmured Johnny. "And I would
sure like to know what happened to my guitar."

Aelric left his followers to fly into town. Once there he headed straight for the reference section of the public library. It was a struggle for a small fairy to take a book from the shelves and read it, and liable to cause panic among customers, but Aelric was badly in need of information.

He was stuck for inspiration as to what to do next in his guerrilla war against King Tala. Guerrilla warfare did not come naturally to peaceful Cornish fairies, and he and his small band of followers had to fight continually against the urge to walk up to Tala and say something like, "Look, we're all fairies here. Let's be reasonable about this." Tala was a new type of oppressive fairy, and not to be reasoned with.

Aelric hunted out the political philosophy section and dragged out a summary of the works of Chairman Mao.

"Hi, I'm Linda, and me and my friend do the hottest two-girl phone sex in town—"

"Why do you spend your time watching this ridiculous sex channel?"

"I do not spend time watching it. I was just flicking through the channels and it came on."

Heather laughed.

"I have an urge to hear some Scottish music. Let us go and find some musicians."

"No one plays Scottish music in New York. Only Irish."

"Really? I am surprised. But never mind, it's much the same. We taught them everything they know. Where can we hear some?"

Dinnie knew of a bar on Fourteenth and Ninth where there were regular sessions, but he had no enthusiasm for the journey. Heather nagged him.

"It's all very well you burbling on about jigs and reels," said Dinnie crossly. "But how am I to enjoy listening to music when

I am going to be evicted tomorrow? No thanks to you."

Heather frowned.

"Let me get this straight, Dinnie, because I am not sure that I quite understand it. You have to give that man money every week to live here. You have failed to do this for five weeks. Consequently he has told you to leave. Am I right so far?"

"Dead on."

"So," continued Heather, "all that is required is for you to get a bundle of those dollar things and give it to the man. Then everything will be all right."

"Yes, you dumb fairy, but I don't have any of those dollar things."

"What about when you went to the cycle courier place? Didn't you earn enough to pay the rent?"

Dinnie snorted.

"I didn't earn enough to buy a pizza."

"Would a pizza do instead of the rent?"

Dinnie clutched his brow.

"Please leave me alone. I can't stand any fairy stupidity right now."

Heather took out her sword and posed briefly in front of the mirror. She made a minor adjustment to her kilt, and smiled.

"Well, as you will realize by now, there is no limit to the ingenuity and resourcefulness of a thistle fairy. Take me to hear the music and I will find money for the rent."

Heather still did not fully understand why you had to pay dollars to live in a dirty room—a very strange business it seemed to her—but she was willing to help.

Heather enjoyed herself at the session. She sneered only occasionally at the human musicians, who were really very skillful, as they sat round the table at one end of the bar, wreathed in cigarette smoke. It was delightful to hear the pipes, whistles, violins, mandolins, banjos and bodrans, and she stamped her bare feet on the table in time to the jigs and reels. Though she and Morag were bent on radicalizing Scottish fairy music, she was still fond of tradition.

When the musicians played some hornpipes, "The Boys of Bluehill" and "Harvest Home," young and old Irish descendants and expatriates left their Guinness and Jamesons to get up and dance in formation.

"I'm touched," said Heather, watching them go round.

"Why?"

"Because they're thinking of home."

Italian fairies are friends with the wind, and skillful at riding on its back.

Three of them rode now on the breeze over Houston Street, just north of their home in Little Italy. They studied the streets to the north and waited.

"There," said the youngest, and pointed. "There she is. Sitting on the shoulder of that large round person."

Dinnie was trudging down Broadway with his eyes fixed firmly on the ground. He was depressed, humiliated and angry.

"I'm sorry," said Heather, for the twentieth time. Dinnie ignored her. He also ignored the beggars, lovers and partygoers who walked beside them in the dark.

"It was a brave attempt," continued the fairy. "It was worth trying. Next time will be better."

Dinnie said that there was not going to be a next time. There would not have been a first time if Heather had not blackmailed him into playing by threatening to make herself visible to the whole audience and create a scene. After a few whiskies she had decided it would be a very good thing if Dinnie showed off his new skill at the fiddle, but it had been a complete disaster. Fingers stiffened by nerves, he had scraped and scratched his way through two strathspeys in the most amateurish way imaginable, all the time surrounded by experienced musicians who did not know whether to grin or look away in embarrassment.

When his dreadful rendition of the tunes finished, there had been a deathly hush. Even the uncontrollable drunk at the next table had quieted. No one in the audience had ever heard such bad playing in public; the session had never seen anything like it. Generally thick-skinned, Dinnie had never before realized that such humiliation was possible.

Dinnie told Heather that there would not be a next time because he was never going to play the violin again, either in public or private. Furthermore, he would appreciate it if she would now find somewhere else to live and leave him alone. For the rest of his life.

When he tramped past a honey-roasted peanut vendor's stall without even a hungry glance, Heather knew that things were serious.

"Do not be so down-hearted," she pleaded. "Everyone has to start somewhere. I'm sorry I made you play before you were ready. I know it was a mistake. I understand that you are embarrassed. But all those good players were once beginners too. They know what it's like."

"They didn't have a fairy blackmailing them into playing before they were ready and making a fool of themselves in public."

Heather had to admit that this was probably true.

"But I can make it up to you. I have the money for the rent." She brought a bundle of tightly folded dollars out of her sporran and handed it to Dinnie.

He took it in silence. Even rescue from eviction could not cheer him up after his embarrassment.

"Where did you get this," he asked, back in his room.

"Fairy magic," lied Heather.

Dinnie switched on the TV.

"I'll lick your asshole and you can bang mine," crooned a naked woman with long dark hair, kneeling over a couch. "Only twelve dollars for three minutes."

"I did not entirely understand that," said Heather, trying to start a conversation. "Is it connected with the nice, young, pink, warm, juicy pussies?"

Dinnie ignored her completely.

The Italian fairies made their way home.

"She handed him the stolen money."

"What does this mean? Who is she?"

The Italian fairies did not know. They had heard rumors of some disturbance with the Chinese fairies who lived not far away, and wondered if it was something to do with them. It was a long time since there had been any contact with them, but some distant suspicion, born of old, still lingered.

Whatever it meant, they were most unhappy that a strange fairy had boldly gone into an Italian bank, picked the lock of the vault and made off with a sporran full of money.

TEN

Kerry and Morag hunted the Lower East Side for the poppy with no success. After Cal's criminal act of removing it from her apartment then leaving it in the theater, it had vanished.

Morag made efforts to lighten Kerry's mood by working out the guitar parts on "Born to Lose," a Johnny Thunders classic, but neither Kerry's heart nor her fingers were in it. All she felt like doing was drinking beer.

Heather was most perturbed at Dinnie's refusal to play his fiddle. If she failed in her attempt to teach him, then Morag would subject her to terrible ridicule. Terrible ridicule from Morag was more than Heather could bear. She was already dreading that her rival might learn of the debacle at the session.

"Why did I ever brag to that foul MacPherson that I would teach this useless lump to play? I was taken in by the beauty of his fiddle. It has the most exquisite tone, but I have staked my clan pride on an imbecile."

"Come on Dinnie, practice."

"No."

"If you don't practice, Morag MacPherson will mock me

and all the MacKintoshes," cried the fairy in frustration.

"Aha!" said Dinnie. "So that's why you're so keen for me to learn. I might have known you had an ulterior motive. Well, I don't give a shit about the MacKintoshes, or the MacPhersons."

Heather swallowed her outrage and spoke sweetly. She pleaded, persuaded, whined, nagged, flattered and cajoled him, finally appealing to his vanity by telling him that with his fiddle under his chin, he really was a fine figure of a man.

"Do you really think so?"

Heather nodded. "Most attractive."

Dinnie grinned, and Heather knew that she had found a weak spot. One of Dinnie's most profound desires was to be attractive.

"I shouldn't doubt," she continued, "that if you learn a few more tunes and go back to that session, the young Irish colleens will be clustering round you in no time. Even last week I noticed a few of them eyeing you."

Dinnie picked up his fiddle.

I have exceeded myself, thought Heather. I have finally made him love the fiddle. She tripped happily downstairs on her way to the bar. Cal was on the steps, talking to a young woman.

"You will be a great Titania," he said. "Come and audition. You'll love it. You get to be the Fairy Queen on a stage strewn with flowers."

The mention of flowers made Heather think of her estranged friend Morag. They had both been very friendly with flowers in Scotland. She decided to fly across the road and see what she was up to.

Across the road, Morag and Kerry were listening to old Lydia Lunch tapes and drinking beer. Kerry told Morag about her childhood in Maine, and her parents, who had died when she was young, leaving her nothing but a large health-insurance policy, which turned out to be very fortunate.

"And since then I have been poor. I have tried making money from my art here in New York but without much success. It is very dispiriting."

Kerry's last artistic effort had been a commission from friends of Cal to draw an album cover for them for a record they were putting out with their own money.

"I drew a beautiful woman, based on Botticelli's Venus – similar to me in fact – lying on a bed of rose petals. It was lovely, but the band said it didn't go with the album's title."

"What was that?"

"*Rock Me, Fuck Me, Kill Me.* Lousy record."

This had been Kerry's last commercial enterprise. Since then, she had been living on virtually no money. Now that Morag was here to help with the shoplifting and till robbing for the rent, things were a little easier.

"Now, Morag, where am I going to find a red, yellow and orange Welsh poppy? Without that flower the alphabet will not be complete and it must be complete if I am going to beat Cal in the competition."

At the mention of Cal, Kerry threw down her Indian headband in fury. Not only had he rejected her because of her colostomy bag, he had also sabotaged her flowers.

Magenta arrived at a small park in Houston Street and sat down to consult her copy of Xenophon. A few pigeons meandered around, picking up crumbs. Before she could begin reading she was interrupted by a tramp who knew her well. He took some time off from washing windshields at the traffic lights and sauntered over.

"What you got there? Xenophon?" He burst out laughing. "Xenophon is a pile of crap. All the most recent literary-archeological authorities show that he was not as important in the expedition as he made out."

Magenta did not stop to listen anymore. She checked that her new booty, a priceless triple-bloomed flower, was safely tucked in her shopping bag and marched off.

"Wait till Joshua catches up with you!" he shouted after her.

"I see a sewage spill closed three Long Island beaches yesterday. Also Nassau County health authority received a flurry of calls from people who became ill after eating contaminated clams."

Morag was reading a newspaper after a Kerry attempt at a guitar solo had ended in defeat. She was persistent in her love of the New York Dolls, though, and would never entirely give up.

"And a Brooklyn teenager was stabbed to death in Sunset Park after an argument."

"Mmmm."

"And two muggers went on a crime spree in Midtown, doing three knife-point robberies in five minutes."

Kerry grimaced.

"Perhaps you should tell me a tale about Scotland instead."

"If you absolutely insist."

Morag swallowed an oatcake, washed it down with a little beer and began.

"James MacPherson was a famous Scottish robber and a great fiddle player. He was afraid of no one and his exploits were legendary, but eventually he was captured by treachery in Keith market. This was around 1700, I think. MacPherson was a good friend of the fairies and even had a happy relationship with a mermaid, which is sort of a fairy.

"Now, the most famous fiddle-maker of the MacPherson fairies, Red Dougal MacPherson, lived around then, and he was very fond of MacPherson the Robber. They used to drink and play music together in the hills around Banff. Red Dougal taught James many fairy fiddling techniques and it is said that no fiddling duo before or since could match them. In return for this, MacPherson the Robber used to bring Red Dougal and the other MacPherson fairies great skins of whisky and choice jewels from his robbing.

"Eventually they were such good friends that Red Dougal made a violin with all his skill and craft and took it to the great Annie MacPherson, who was head of the MacPherson fairy clan. She gave the fiddle shape-changing powers so it could become big enough for a human to play, and Red Dougal presented it to James.

"The instrument had a matchless tone. In the right hands it could hypnotize an audience. It could make you laugh or cry. It could send warriors marching through the glens or send a baby to sleep. It was famous throughout Scotland, and although MacPherson carried it with him, it was counted as one of the three great Scottish fairy artifacts, and belonged to the clan as a whole.

"Then MacPherson the Robber was betrayed and captured and sentenced to death by the sheriff. He was locked up in prison in Banff. The fairies tried to free him but the sheriff was too strong with English magic and we could do nothing. MacPherson sat in his cell and composed one last tune, the famous 'MacPherson's Lament.'"

"Annie MacPherson did manage, through her great power, to secure a pardon for the robber, and this would have pleased all the Scottish folk, for he never robbed the poor, only the rich. But the sheriff knew the reprieve was on its way and cunningly moved the town clock up an hour. So the execution went ahead an hour early, and the reprieve arrived too late.

"When James MacPherson stood on the gallows he played the tune he'd composed in his cell, the "MacPherson's Lament." MacPherson fairies were watching and they remembered the tune, which is how it still survives. Then the robber smashed his fiddle to bits over his knee in anger and cried his defiance to the world. After that he was hanged.

"And that was the end of the same MacPherson fiddle. No one even knew what happened to the pieces."

Heather crouched outside Kerry's second floor window, listening.

"A terrible shame it was lost," Morag was saying, "because Red Dougal was the best fairy violin maker that ever graced the country, and by all accounts the MacPherson Fiddle was the finest instrument he ever made."

Outside the window Heather clutched her brow. She was awestruck. She raced back to Dinnie's rooms.

It had been a puzzle to Heather why Dinnie's fiddle had such a stirring tone, even in the hands of such a bad player, and she had just had a startling psychic insight, which she was not at all famous for.

"Dinnie! This is none other than the legendary fairy instrument, the MacPherson Fiddle."

Dinnie lounged in front of the TV and paid Heather no attention.

"Oh baby, I'd love to suck your hard cock," cooed a woman in a bikini down a red phone. Call 970 S-U-C-K for the hottest phone sex in town."

I might have to kill this person some time, thought Heather.

Morag rode, walked and fluttered through the city, but failed to find any trace of Kerry's missing flower. The competition was less than three weeks away. There was only one thing to do. She climbed a fire escape, looked up at the sky, and prayed to

Dianna, Goddess of the Fairies.

When she glided back down to street level, there was Magenta, marching towards her, and poking out of her shopping bag was the preserved bloom.

"Thank you, Dianna," said Morag, and materialized.

She briefly explained about the flower and asked for it back.

Magenta fled, calling orders for her troops to form a square, archers and horsemen at the rear.

"Could we possibly find another one somewhere?" asked Morag, back at Kerry's.

"No," said Dinnie. "No, no, no. You can't have it."

He grabbed hold of the violin.

"But you don't even like it."

"Yes I do. It makes me attractive. Young Irish girls will soon be flocking round. You said so yourself."

Heather glowered in hopeless frustration. She had made Dinnie love his instrument, and now she needed it.

"Anyway," protested Dinnie. "I don't believe you. How can this be the famous MacPherson Fiddle, whatever that is."

"It's one of Scotland's most famous fairy icons. I don't know how it ended up in New York, but it has. I recognize its tone. Any Scottish fairy would. Except we all thought it was lost centuries ago. I must have it. If I go back to Scotland with the MacPherson Fiddle, I will be forgiven for the damage I did to the MacLeod banner."

"How could it be a fairy instrument? It's too big."

"It's a shape-changing instrument."

"It would be."

Dinnie and Heather glared at each other.

"I could steal it."

"No you couldn't," Dinnie said triumphantly. "You're a

good fairy. You're not allowed to steal a human's favorite thing. Especially not a fellow MacKintosh's."

Heather thought frantically. What did fairies do when they needed something from a human and were unable to steal it? Of course. They bargained.

"I'll trade you for it."

Cal was suffering from stress. Trying to put on a production of *A Midsummer Night's Dream* on a minimal budget was proving to be extremely difficult. To make things worse, he seemed to have landed himself with a highly strung group of performers, and interruptions from mad bag ladies were more than they could cope with.

He plugged in his guitar to relax. Cal was a good guitarist. He could play almost anything; he could play along to the noise of the traffic, or the rattle from his air conditioner.

He played through some riffs and chord sequences, then his fingers slid easily over some of his favorite guitar solos.

He frowned. Playing old New York Dolls guitar solos made him feel slightly guilty, since he had promised to teach them to Kerry, then left her before doing so.

"Listen," said Johnny, up in Heaven.

"What?" said Billy.

"Somewhere down there. They're still playing my stuff."

Johnny Thunders and Billy Murcia, deceased members of the New York Dolls, picked up the vague vibrations of the lead break from "Rock and Roll Nurse."

"I really wish I knew what happened to my guitar," repeated Johnny. "I miss that Gibson Tiger Top. There was never another one like it. Even here I can't find a replacement."

Across the blessed heavenly field from them, Chinese spirits were still making their preparations to visit earth for the Festival of Hungry Ghosts.

"A thistle fairy engaged in a trade is empowered to offer any-thing," claimed Heather. "Just name it."

Dinnie looked at Heather suspiciously.

"Okay," he said. "I'll give you it for a million dollars."

"Eh, well, I can't really do that."

"Ha! I knew you were lying."

Heather fluttered around in agitation.

"I was not lying. I can trade you anything. Except money. We are not allowed to bargain with wealth. Sorry."

"You paid my rent."

"That was helping a human in need. Not a bargain."

"Well, to hell with you. I'll keep the violin."

"Oh, come on, there must be something else you want. I can get you your heart's desire."

Dinnie wandered over to the window. He couldn't think what his heart desired and he had no wish to give up his fiddle.

"I don't want anything. So you can't have it. Now excuse me, I'm off to buy some beer. And let this be a lesson to you. You fairies might think you're smart, but compared to a human like me, you're nowhere."

Dinnie, vastly pleased at putting one over on Heather, whom he regarded as altogether too pushy for her own good, hummed a tune as he waddled down the stairs.

In Cornwall, Magris was not pleased. King Tala had instructed him to bring back Petal and Tulip. In Magris's eyes, this was a waste of time. They were far away and could do no harm.

Magris was more interested in his restructuring of Cornish fairy society. Already, under his guidance, the fairies no longer lived free in the woods but were concentrated in workhouses under the rule of barons. As a consequence of this, production had soared and trade with the fairies in France and elsewhere was booming. As far as he could see, the only problem facing them was Aelric and his band, and he had every confidence that they would soon be apprehended by the security forces.

"I have moved you overnight from being the nominal lord of a hunter-gatherer society into the king of a well-ordered feudal realm," he told Tala. "And now that I have invented the steam engine, there is no limit to our progress. We will make as many goods as the humans. Forget Tulip and Petal, they are not important."

Tala, however, was set in his ways and would not accept their flight. He ordered Magris to bring them back. So Magris sent messengers with gold to gather a band of mercenaries, and thought about the most efficient way of sending them to America.

Kerry and Morag were buying coffee and beer in the deli.

"What's that noise?"

There was a distant hum which grew quickly into a loud bustle of shouting and marching as a large procession turned onto Fourth Street and tramped its way along.

"It's a protest march."

"What's it about?"

"We're here, we're queer, get used to it!" chanted the procession.

The marchers stretched out their arms through the ranks of the surrounding police to give out leaflets detailing their grievances. Kerry took a leaflet and read it to Morag. It said that in recent weeks there had been an increase in attacks on gays in the city. Men were waiting outside gay nightclubs and bars and harassing anyone who came out. This had led to serious injuries and the gay community was protesting that they were not receiving enough protection from the police.

"We're here, we're queer, get used to it!"

The men and women marching were mainly young and they were grim faced. Scores of police officers surrounded them and roughly shepherded them along. Not far away, in Tomkins Square, there had been a series of disturbances and as the demonstration was heading that way the police were handling the crowd.

Kerry saw faces she recognized and waved to the marchers. She told Morag that only last week two friends of hers had been beaten up after leaving a gay bar in the West Village.

Morag was perplexed by the whole thing. Kerry did her best to explain it to her but she was a little disconcerted when Morag burst out laughing.

"What's funny?"

"You humans," shrieked Morag and laughed uproariously. "You make such silly problems for yourselves. We fairies have no such difficulties. Even the MacKintoshes, who are thieves cheats and liars, have more sense than to take any notice of two men fairies rolling round in the glens."

"These glens are sounding more and more interesting," said Kerry. "You must take me there some time."

"Get out of my way, you damned faggots," sounded a rough voice nearby. "Can't a man go out for a beer these days without being apprehended by a bunch of pansy radicals?"

It was Dinnie, elbowing his way to the deli.

"Hello, Dinnie," said Kerry. Dinnie seemed taken aback, and spluttered. He walked off without replying.

"We're going in the wrong direction," said Heather, on his shoulder. "And why are you blushing?"

Back in his apartment Dinnie poured beer down his throat and Heather sniggered.

"You are in love with Kerry."

"Don't be ridiculous," snorted Dinnie.

"I'm not being ridiculous. I saw you blush, stammer and

walk away in the wrong direction after she said hello. You can't fool a fairy about this sort of thing.

"Well, Dinnie, this is your lucky day. Bringing lovers together is a particular specialty of mine. No case too hopeless. And this can be our bargain. You give me the MacPherson Fiddle, and I will get you Kerry."

Dinnie was more than dubious about Heather's proposal. He dismissed it as preposterous.

"There's nothing preposterous about it. It's a braw scheme. The best I ever had. You give me the fiddle and I give you Kerry.

"Think of the advantages. Once you are going out with Kerry, everybody will want to be your friend because she is immensely popular and any man she chooses to go out with must be a fairly desirable specimen. Virtually overnight you will be transformed from a lonely and pathetic creature, despised by all, into a hip young man about town with a cool girlfriend. Instead of wallowing about in an armchair every night watching baseball and sex programs you will be able to turn up at gigs and nightclubs with Kerry on your arm, making everyone jealous. She is a most attractive young woman, and highly desirable. Your happiness will be unbounded.

"As for me, once I have the MacPherson Fiddle, I will be changed from a wanted outlaw to Scotland's most popular fairy. Returning home with such a famous and long-lost item will stun and amaze the whole of fairydom and more than make up for the accident with the banner. It will sink into the heads of even the ignorant MacLeods that I am a fairy to be feted and honored, rather than chased with knives and claymores over Ben Lomord."

Heather shuddered at the memory of this particularly unpleasant incident.

"And even if it doesn't sink into their heads, such a heroic act would place me under the protection of Mavis, the Scottish Fairy Queen. I would be safe and welcome everywhere."

Heather glowed at the thought of returning in triumph to her clan lands around Tomatin. If the famous and revered MacPherson Fiddle was returned to Scotland by her, a MacKintosh, it would shut the MacPhersons up in a spectacular manner, and keep them in their proper place for ages to come. She might even be able to get the judges' decision at the junior fiddling contest re-examined, forcing them to admit that her version of "Tullochgorum" was better than Morag's.

And for another thing, Dinnie dating Kerry would upset Morag to no end. The way Morag had been able to brag that her human friend was popular, attractive and a bundle of fun while Heather's was a sort of human slug had been most annoying. What would Morag say when her popular attractive friend fell hopelessly for the majestic Dinnie MacKintosh, pride of his clan?

Dinnie agreed to the bargain; Heather chuckled in anticipation.

Kerry crossed the road to the theater. Morag picked the lock and they snuck in. Once inside, Kerry destroyed all the props for *A Midsummer Night's Dream*. She sliced up the costumes with a knife and broke all the scenery with a hammer.

"Feeling better?" asked Morag, back at the flat.

"A little," replied Kerry. "Now, what should I pin in my hair? A rose or a carnation?"

Morag gave this her deepest consideration, but it was a tough question.

"What flower do you need next?"

They were pressing on with the alphabet in the hope that they would somehow recover the most important flower.

Kerry consulted her book.

"A bright orange Eschscholzia. Grows in California. That shouldn't be too difficult."

Heather journeyed down to the small park on Houston Street to give the matter of Dinnie's romance her best consideration.

Below her on the street, groups of young people wandered by on their way to a gig at the Knitting Factory. Studying them, Heather appreciated that they were not really the same as the young people she had been acquainted with in her small village.

Perhaps I should do a little background research before deciding on how to bring them together, she thought. I am in a strange city and I do not want to waste my time getting Dinnie to do all the wrong things. For instance, a gift of oatcakes, while guaranteed to win over a Highland fairy, may not have the same potency in New York. I will need to plan carefully.

Pleased with her astute reasoning, she fluttered into the air and headed off to do a little research.

Dinnie, unusually, never ate out. He did not like to waste time in restaurants but bought the cheapest things he could fry easily on his little cooker. He passed a quiet evening eating corned-beef hash and watching quiz shows and wondered if Heather could indeed do as she promised. Although he had no intention of admitting it to Heather, he had never had a girlfriend. It did not seem possible that his first one would be the much sought-after Kerry.

In the happy aura created by Heather and Morag's presence, the two tramps on the stairs passed into deep dreams of pleasant places, places so wondrous that they did not want to come back.

"Hi, Dinnie," said Heather, performing a happy somersault on the windowsill. "I'm back. I have considered the matter and I have it well in hand."

Dinnie blushed.

"And," said Heather, bounding onto Dinnie's shoulder, "I

have worked out a complete plan of action. Guaranteed to make Kerry fall in love with you."

Dinnie sneered.

"Don't sneer. I can do it. I made you play a difficult strathspey, didn't I? A next-to-impossible task, your playing being what it was. Well, I can get you Kerry."

Heather hopped right onto Dinnie's head, which he particularly hated, and peered down over his forehead.

"Now do not think, Dinnie, that I am underestimating the problem? I am well aware that the chances of you capturing Kerry's heart would seem extremely slim. Possibly nonexistent. She is, after all, a highly desirable young lady with practically everything going for her, while you are a fat lump without any notably attractive features."

"Thanks a lot," muttered Dinnie.

"Also, do not think I am unaware of the social mores of New York. I am. I know that a gift of oatcakes is not going to have the profound effect here that it might among the fairies of my village. I had one of my most pleasant experiences ever after taking a fellow fairy four oatcakes and a jar of honey. Three weeks of uninterrupted sex and debauchery in a quiet cave. Wonderful. However, things are different here. Kerry is a young rock and roller and we have to act accordingly."

She leapt down onto the table, red and gold hair streaming, face beaming.

"And how do I know all this?" she demanded. "I'll tell you how I know all this. I have spent all afternoon spying on Kerry and her dumb friend Morag, and all evening in the hip cafes of Avenue A listening to the fashionable young people and reading rock and roll magazines. I know what she likes and I know how to make you into it. All that is required is for you to do as I say."

Dinnie remained silent. He was unwilling to believe it. Heather exchanged a few words of gossip with a cockroach that was scuttling its way past the cooker, picking up scraps.

The cooker, uncleaned for years and utterly filthy, was a fertile hunting ground.

"So, Dinnie, here is the bargain. I promise to make Kerry fall in love with you. In return you give me the MacPherson Fiddle. Do you agree?"

Dinnie agreed, even when Heather further informed him that from now on he must do precisely as she instructed, or she would regard the bargain as broken and depart with the fiddle.

"Anyone breaking a bargain with a fairy renders themselves liable to almost anything."

The fairy peered out the window.

"Oh, no," she cried. "I can't believe it. Two more tramps have died on the steps."

Dinnie did not react.

"Do something, Dinnie."

"What?"

"Phone up whoever you phone up in New York when someone dies. I hate the way they just lie there."

Dinnie grunted that it was fine with him if they lay there all year.

"Dinnie. Listen well. From what I have seen of Kerry, apart from being a friend to the accursed MacPherson, she is a kind, warm human being. No doubt she will like men who are also kind, warm human beings. It therefore follows that you are going to become a kind, warm human being. Failing that, you are going to pretend to be one. So get on the phone."

Dinnie did as he was told.

ELEVEN

Morag hopped in Kerry's window with an Eschscholzia bloom and a troubled look.

"Found this at a flower stall in Midtown," she muttered, then proceeded to tell Kerry a sorry tale.

"I saw a young child crying after dropping her lollipop in the gutter. Naturally, I materialized in front of her to cheer her up. In Scotland this would have met with total approval, shouts of glee from the child and suchlike. Unfortunately in New York it didn't. She got a fright and jumped backward into the street."

Morag frowned.

"It takes a terrible long time for an ambulance to arrive in this city."

Kerry sympathized, and said at least she had meant well, but Morag could not be easily consoled. She had caused a serious accident which was bad enough, but she was convinced something terrible would happen to her in return. According to Morag, fairy karma was notoriously powerful.

Still, there was nothing to do but press on with today's program, which was to track down the young bag lady in possession of the triple-bloomed Welsh poppy.

The afternoon was uncomfortably hot. Magenta sat down to rest at the corner of Avenue C and Fourth. Today, by her reckoning, she had marched forty parsangs under continued harassment from Tissaphernes. This lieutenant of Antaxerxes was a crafty opponent, content at this stage to harry her troops while avoiding a direct frontal attack. This was just as well for both sides really, as Xenophon's Greek Hoplites were immeasurably more disciplined than the Persians' and would inflict dreadful casualties if attacked, but this deep inside enemy territory the Persian's greater number would tell in the end.

A fire truck wailed by. Magenta ignored it and scanned the rooftops for hidden archers. Finding none, she took a swig of her drink and allowed herself a short sleep outside a little hall with a banner over the door.

Kerry busied herself with the bag at her side. There is no known cause for Crohn's disease, and no known cure, so when Morag asked Kerry if she would one day get better, Kerry could only reply that she might.

"I might heal up inside and then the doctors could give me a reversal operation and I wouldn't have to have a colostomy bag anymore. Or I might stay just the same for a long time, which would still not be well enough to be fixed. Or I might have more attacks and have to get more of my intestines removed and then I would never be able to have a reversal operation."

This was always enough to bring a tear to Kerry's eye and Morag would generally have to change the subject.

Kerry hunted among the bundles on the floor for all her brightest garments—her long ragged yellow skirt, her sweatshirt dyed red, blue, pink and purple, her green Indian waistcoat covered with embroidery and mirror fragments, her beads and headband, round sunglasses tinted blue, fringed suede bag with more embroidery, baseball boots splashed with the entire contents of a junior painting kit and a carnation to pin in her hair.

"Would the rose be better?"

"I still can't make up my mind," said Morag. "Have you considered daisies?"

"Let's go."

Outside, Kerry, who was regularly whistled and shouted at by men in the street, suffered a prolonged stream of unpleasant catcalls when she passed by a gang of construction workers. She did not like this but did not answer back.

"I'd like to get between the cheeks of your tight ass!"

"How depressing," said Morag, on her shoulder. "Perhaps this is the start of my bad karma."

Kerry assured her that it was not, as it happened to her all the time.

In the hot sun pedestrians toiled along unhappily and the traffic everywhere was tangled and congested. It did not feel like a good day.

As Kerry and Morag reached Avenue B, scene of Morag's sighting of Magenta, a car made a violent maneuver onto the sidewalk in an attempt to break free of a traffic jam and Kerry was forced to leap for her life. Morag tumbled into a doorway and landed heavily.

"My karma," she wailed.

"I'm sure it's just a coincidence," said Kerry, and brushed the dirt off the fairy's kilt. Morag was not convinced, and when on the next corner two crazed skateboarders forced Kerry to leap briskly for cover, sending Morag once more plummeting groundwards, the fairy declared that she would be doing well if she were still alive at the end of the day.

"Change, any change?"

Kerry brought out some change, gave it to the beggar, apologized for not having any Botticelli postcards on her, and scanned the horizon. A flowerpot tumbled from somewhere above and missed her by inches.

Kerry was shaken.

"Can't you do anything about this, Morag?"

"There is only one possibility. I shall have to perform some immense good deed and work off the bad karma."

They looked around for some good deed to do, but none was in view.

"I'll just have to wait it out," whispered Morag, "and hope I get the chance before some more terrible occurrence overwhelms me."

Dinnie and Heather met Cal as they left the theater. Cal's arms were full of flowers. He nodded to Dinnie pleasantly.

"Coming to see *A Midsummer Night's Dream*?"

"Damned fairy rubbish," replied Dinnie pointedly. "And how about not making so much noise when you rehearse."

"Who was that," asked Heather, following Dinnie on his mission to buy beer.

"Cal. Big mouth big shot of the community theater downstairs. He's got some stupid idea to put on a show and play all the music on his guitar. The whole thing will be a disaster. He only wants to meet young actresses and fuck them."

Magenta woke, sensing danger.

"There she is," cried Morag.

Magenta bolted into the hall behind her.

Kerry and Morag hurried after her, but inside what turned out to be a small gallery there were so many people it was difficult to move and their quarry was nowhere in sight.

This was a fundraising event with many local artists exhibiting their work and local poets doing readings. It was meant to be fun, but as today was intolerably hot it seemed more like an ordeal for everyone.

Trapped in the crowd, Magenta nowhere in sight, Kerry and Morag could only stand and strain their necks to see what was going on.

A young red-haired woman mounted the stage.

"I know her," whispered Kerry.

It was Gail, a friend of hers, about to read her poems.

Unfortunately by this time no one was paying attention to anything anymore, except sweating and wondering whether to leave.

"Oh dear," muttered Kerry. "Everyone is fed up with the heat and the crush and will not listen to Gail, even though she is a great poet."

As Kerry had predicted, few people paid attention. It was just too uncomfortable to listen to poetry, or anything. Morag saw her chance to undo her bad karma. She unwrapped her fiddle and played, just on the threshold of human hearing. The effect was immediate. The audience was hypnotized by Gail's words and fairy music. They quieted down and listened, transfixed.

When Gail read a poem of sadness, Morag played a lament and it was as much as anyone could do to keep from crying. Gail read a fierce poem about property developers moving into the area and chasing out the poor, and Morag played a stirring strathspey. When this was over the audience was on the point of storming the property developers' offices and running them out of town. Gail finished with a love poem, and Morag played "My Love Is Like A Red, Red Rose," and everyone in the crowd felt that they were definitely in love with someone, and it was going to work out well.

As she finished there was wild uncontrollable applause. Gail smiled. She had been a huge success. Morag smiled as well. This successful good deed would surely have worked off her bad karma.

"There she is," cried Kerry, sighting Magenta in the distance, and hurried off. Morag made to follow but the man next to her, clapping his hand furiously, knocked the fiddle onto the floor. It was invisible to him and he stamped on it.

Kerry found Magenta as she was about to make her getaway and retrieved her flower with a determined frontal assault. Later she placed the bloom back in its place as pride of her collection. She was happy now, but Morag was inconsolable.

They looked at the shattered violin.

"This is the worst day of my life," said Morag.

TWELVE

Spiro the squirrel ceased chewing a nut to peer at Maeve. "Why are you sad?"

"I miss Ireland," she replied, and Padraig nodded in agreement. They regretted the day they had ever hopped on the ferry to England just to find out what it was like.

"And why are you sad, Petal and Tulip?"

"We are scared that our father the King will find us even here and make us go back," they said.

"Does he know how to get on a jumbo jet?"

"Magris knows everything," said Brannoc, and thought about killing him.

In the distance some joggers panted their way through a long circuit of the park.

"Play us some music," said Spiro. "The whole park has seemed more peaceful since you've been here. Play some music and I will show you where to find the largest mushrooms this side of the Atlantic."

So the fairies played in Central Park and the animals and humans stopped to listen. Radios were turned down and children stopped screaming. The joggers, bikers and baseball players took a rest. Everyone who heard went home happy and stayed happy for the whole day. No one fought or argued and no crimes were committed while the park fairies played.

Cornwall was less happy.

"I cannot have my son and daughter escaping the country," said Tala the King. "It will give encouragement to the resistance groups."

Magris shrugged. He was more interested in inventing new and efficient machines for producing goods.

"I could try opening up a moonbow between here and New York. But generating enough power to send a full host will take time."

Tala was impatient with this. He wanted his children back now.

"Do you have enough power to send over a smaller force?"

Magris nodded.

"Very well. Assemble some mercenaries."

Tala had a gold crown of the finest workmanship. He also had twelve powerful barons controlling the Cornish fairy population. This meant that his crown was not quite as powerful as it used to be. However, with his mind concentrated on the greatly increased production which Magris's reorganization of their society had brought, he did not yet realize this.

Due now at a meeting with the barons, he walked through a corridor of small trees but was halted on the way by a messenger with the shocking news that Aelric and his band of resistance fighters had set fire to the royal granary, thereby destroying the king's food store, and that of his court. This grain would have to be replaced by one of the barons, which would cause hardship in his territory.

Magris held a propaganda leaflet, distributed by Aelric. It urged Cornish fairies everywhere to throw off their chains and support the beloved Petal and Tulip as new rulers of the kingdom.

"The rebels tried to distribute them," Magris told the King. "Fortunately our troops prevented it."

"This Aelric must be caught," raged the King, and he gave instructions that the strongest fliers among his army must be sent to guard his installations from the air, so that the harmful propaganda leaflets could not be dropped.

"I must have some whisky," said Padraig, laying down his fiddle, and no one disagreed with him. It was a long time since any of the Central Park fairies had had a drink. The squirrels, friendly though they were, could not be persuaded to bring them any. They said it was too dangerous an endeavor. This particularly disgusted Maeve.

"Back in Ireland," she told the others, "a squirrel would go out of its way to bring a fairy some poteen. Although normally the problem would not arise as the humans there are good, friendly folk and generally leave it lying around for us."

There was nothing for it but to mount an expedition to the streets beyond the park.

"We'll hit the first bar we see."

The loss of the triple-bloomed Welsh poppy, so soon after its dramatic recovery, was a shattering blow to Kerry. She stared furiously at the ransom note from the Chinese fairies.

"How dare they hold my flower hostage!"

Kerry saw her ambitions crumbling into nothing. Without the Welsh poppy she could not win the East Fourth Street Community Arts Prize and without Morag's fiddle she could not learn any Johnny Thunders guitar solos.

"I have made up my mind," said Johnny Thunders. "I can never be satisfied, even here in Heaven, until I know what happened to my 1958 Gibson Tiger Top. I just laid it down on a barstool for a minute in CBGB's and when I turned around it was gone. And there never was another guitar like it."

Billy Murcia nodded sympathetically.

"And I sure could do with my best guitar right now," added Johnny. "Because as far as I can find out, there is an acute short-age of good rock bands around here. Plenty hippies and plenty gospel choirs, but nothing gritty. So when these Chinese spirits head on out for the Festival of Hungry Ghosts, I'm going with them."

The fairies from Central Park ventured warily into the streets.

"That looks like a bar," hissed Brannoc after a while, although they found it difficult to tell. The buildings were all so different from the small Cornish and Irish dwellings they were used to. Because of this uncertainty they had traveled farther into Harlem than they intended and were now well out of sight of the park.

People were everywhere on these streets and traffic belched fumes that made the fairies' eyes sting. They were all nervous, though Brannoc and Maeve refused to show it. Pausing to let four small children with a huge radio scurry past, they made ready to invade the bar.

"Fill your bottles with whisky and pouches with tobacco as fast as you can, then get out of here. The sooner we're back in the park the better."

"Harlem's Friendliest Bar," said a newly painted sign out-side. They hurried in. The bar was quiet. A few customers sat with beers, watching the television up on the wall. Unseen, the fairies set to work. They pressed their wine skins to the whisky optics and gathered up tobacco from behind the bar.

"Just like the time we raided O'Shaugnessy's in Dublin," whispered Maeve, and Padraig managed a nervous grin.

"And did we not get ruined that night!"

It was a smooth operation. Within minutes the five of them

were gathered at the door ready to return to their sanctuary.

"Everyone ready?" said Brannoc. "Okay, let's go."

"Correct me if I'm wrong," said a voice behind them, "but have you just been robbing this bar?"

They spun around, shocked. Standing there were two black fairies, and they did not seem at all pleased.

Unaware of the otherworldly drama on the sidewalk, humans walked back and forth. A group of three men, fresh from a meeting concerning the setting up of a fund to help destitute former baseball players, strolled into the bar to discuss the day's progress. Two construction workers walked in to spend the rest of the afternoon eking out one beer each, because these days the construction business was terrible.

"Construction spending fell 2.6% last year," it said in their trade paper. No one seemed to have any money to give them work.

The barman sympathized with their troubles. His trade was not good either.

Outside, the fairies fled.

Forty-two mercenaries gathered at nightfall on Bodmin Moor in Cornwall. Magris looked down at them and up at the clouds. Muttering a few words of the old tongue he magicked up a light fall of rain. As a scientist Magris disliked magic, but it had its uses. He waited for the moon to appear.

The mercenaries were homeless fairies from around the British Isles—Scottish Red Caps, English Spriggans, Welsh Bwbachods, and Irish Firbolgs, They stood, silent and grim, and waited. Twenty-one of the mercenaries would begin a determined search-and-destroy mission against Aelric, while the other twenty-one were to cross over to America on the moonbow and capture the fugitives.

Back in Central Park, Tulip was gloomy.

"That was very unfortunate."

"Yes," agreed Petal. "It should have been nice meeting other fairies. I'd no idea there were any."

"I tried my best to be friendly."

"So did I."

"I hated it when they threatened us with death."

They all looked accusingly at Maeve.

"It would have been fine if you had not acted in such a hot-headed manner," said Brannoc angrily.

Maeve tossed her red hair.

"They threatened us. No one threatens an O'Brien fairy"

"Well, it was completely unnecessary to threaten him back with tearing his head off. Is that they way you act in Ireland?"

"Yes."

Brannoc turned away in disgust. The episode had been a disaster. They had succeeded in gathering supplies but, thanks to Maeve's temper, they had alienated a previously unsuspected clan of black fairies.

"They could have been helpful, you know. Now we'll have to avoid them."

Maeve would not give in. She said she did not care how helpful they could have been, no one threatened an O'Brien fairy and got away with it. She drank some whisky and told Brannoc he could go back and make peace if he wanted.

"Though I hope you make a better job of it than the English have done in Ireland so far."

She donned her uillen pipes and started up a jaunty jig to demonstrate her lack of concern. Padraig joined in on his tin whistle, but the tune he introduced was "Banish Misfortune." Although he would not speak against Maeve, he felt that she had not handled things very well. After all, the black fairies did have reason to object. Maeve and he would not have been very

pleased had they found one of their local bars in Galway being
raided by a bunch of strangers.

"Banish Misfortune," is a very lucky jig. Generations of
Celts have played it with optimism, which has given it a magi-
cal power to make things go well. Since ending up in New
York, Padraig had found himself playing it more and more.

The barman in Harlem noticed how empty the whisky bottles
had become.

"We sure sold a lot of Scotch this week," he told the construction workers. "Maybe trade's on the increase after all."

This seemed like heartening news, and the workers were
cheered. In the pleasant afterglows of the fairies' presence, they
felt that better times were bound to come soon.

THIRTEEN

"Dinnie, I have been reading the magazines that were lying in the gutter outside."

"So?"

"Focus your mind carefully on our bargain."

"Why?"

"Because it's time for you to lose weight."

Dinnie gave a yelp. The last thing Dinnie wanted to do was lose weight. Heather knew that this was going to be an awkward beginning to her plan to transform Dinnie, but she was insistent.

"A recent survey in *Cosmopolitan* gave excess weight as the number one turn-off for American women. Kerry is an American woman. It therefore follows that to win her heart you have to lose weight. To put it another way, she is not going to fall for a fat lump like you. So you're going on a diet."

Dinnie spluttered.

"You said you'd make her fall in love with me. You never said anything about making me suffer."

"I said if you did exactly as I said I'd make her fall in love with you. And I say you have to lose weight."

Dinnie immediately refused, but Heather countered by informing him that this would be breaking their bargain and she would now shrink the fiddle to fairy size and remove it.

Dinnie was cornered. He clutched his packet of cookies, panic stricken. He could feel himself going faint as the awful prospect of dieting loomed in front of him.

Heather, not averse to putting one over on Dinnie, smirked maliciously.

"But do not despair, my fat friend. The magazine promised that it is easy to fill yourself up with nourishing and appetizing meals and still lose weight. I have memorized the recipes and you are starting today."

Wails of passion from a rehearsal came up through the floorboards, as Lysander, Demetrius, Hermia and Helena struggled their way through their difficult romance. Dinnie screamed abuse at the performers.

"Now, now," Heather chided him. "Remember that you are also becoming a pleasant and civilized human being. Pleasant and civilized human beings do not scream out to strangers that they are guilty of having sex with their mothers.

"Today's recipe will be nuts and tomatoes. Also, Chinese cabbage leaves, because you need green vegetables. You take a walk to the health food shop on First Avenue for the nuts and buy some tomatoes from the corner shop. Tomatoes are these round red things. I will find the Chinese cabbage leaves because I could do with a little fresh air. While you are at it, keep a lookout for a triple-bloomed Welsh poppy. I have learned that it is most important to Kerry."

Heather hopped onto the windowsill.

"If you get back before me, practice the new jig I showed you, 'The Atholl Highlanders.' It is an extremely fine jig and it is in your book if you can't remember it. Take care not to confuse it with 'The Atholl Volunteers,' 'The Atholl March,' 'Atholl Brose' or 'The Braes of Atholl.' A popular place for songs, Atholl. Cheerio."

The ransom note from the Chinese fairies was a terrible blow to Kerry and Morag.

"GIVE US BACK THE MIRROR OR YOU'LL NEVER SEE YOUR WELSH POPPY AGAIN."

Kerry gazed at it. It seemed to imply magic forces beyond belief.

"How did they get hold of my Welsh Poppy? How did they know where it was? How did they know it was important? And how did they know I had stolen the mirror?"

Morag made a small loop in the air before settling on Kerry's shoulder.

"Fairies can know lots of things by intuition," she explained. "I expect that after they chased me following the regrettable lobster incident, they sensed that I'd been in the shop where the mirror had been. Probably they've been looking for me ever since and when they spotted me they took the first opportunity to burgle your apartment.

"You were wearing your waistcoat today so they couldn't find the mirror, but they took something else. They might have known the Welsh poppy was important to you due to cunning psychic insights. Then again, it might have been because you wrote a sign in red ink above it saying 'This is my most prized possession.'"

Morag volunteered to make the exchange.

"I am sure it will not be too risky. We fairies are reasonable creatures and I will simply explain the whole thing away as a misunderstanding. If that doesn't work, I'll claim you are a kleptomaniac currently undergoing treatment."

"That was the most unpleasant customer I've ever encountered," said an assistant at the health food store to her fellow worker. "You'd think I was twisting his arm to buy a bag of mixed nuts."

"What was it he accused you of?"

"I don't know. It was something about collaborating with fairies to poison the city."

"What a weirdo. Did you notice his coat?"

They shuddered.

Dinnie tramped home. The slight satisfaction of having subjected the sales assistants to some solid abuse had not made him any happier about the day's events.

He flung the nuts on a shelf and settled down for his afternoon nap.

Morag hovered over Canal Street, slightly uncomfortable at the prospect of facing an entire Chinese fairy clan, but confident that things would work out well enough and she would be able to return with Kerry's dried flower. It was desperately important to Morag that Kerry won the Community Arts Prize because this would make her immensely happy, and Morag had read in a medical directory in a bookstore on Second Avenue that being happy was very important to Crohn's disease sufferers. An unhappy Kerry was likely to be a sick Kerry, and a sick Kerry was likely to get more of her insides removed by a surgeon.

Heather, meanwhile, was traveling the short distance to Chinatown to find some Chinese cabbage leaves.

"This is extremely good of me," she thought, idly combing her long hair as a delivery truck took her down Broadway to Canal Street. "I could get him any old cabbage leaves. He'd never know the difference. But the recipe said Chinese, and I am willing to expend effort for a fellow MacKintosh."

She looked up into the dazzling blue sky, and started in surprise. Up above was Morag, surrounded by strange yellow fairies. Heather was not particularly psychic as fairies go, but she easily sensed the hostility of the strangers toward Morag. As she watched, they seemed to be in the process of robbing her of a shining brooch.

Unsheathing her sword and her skian dhu, she flew up into the air.

"Unhand my friend," she screamed, plunging into the floating host, slashing wildly.

Dinnie slumbered peacefully, undisturbed by the four Puerto Rican soccer players on the street below kicking around their tennis ball.

"Raise the clans!" screamed Heather, to Dinnie's immense distress, as she thundered in the window, Morag in tow.

"We're being invaded by a host of yellow fairies!"

"What?"

"Get your sword out. They're attacking over the hills!"

"Will you stop shouting."

"Barricade the doors!" screamed Heather. "Sound the warpipes!"

"Will you shut up, you imbecile!" demanded Dinnie. "What's the idea of bursting in here shouting and screaming. You know I need my afternoon sleep."

"Never mind your sleep. There's yellow fairies with strange weapons massing on the borders."

"Oh, for God's sake, you're not in the Highlands now."

"I had to fight my way out of Canal Street. Only a master swordswoman like myself could have done it. Then we escaped on a police car but they'll be after us. Come on, Morag." She turned to her friend. "Get your sword out."

Heather's mood changed to one of open defiance. She leapt onto the windowsill and began marching up and down.

"Wha daur meddle wi me!" she yelled out the window. "Touch not the cat bot a glove!"

This was the motto of the MacKintosh clan, and obscure even by Scottish standards.

She leaned out to check for the enemy. None were in sight.

"Well," she said. "It seems like I shook them off. Hah! It takes more than a few odd-colored fairies to capture one of the fighting MacKintoshes."

She brandished her sword one last time at the world in general, then hopped back inside.

"Well, Morag, we may have our differences, but never let it be said I was not willing to intervene in a crisis."

Morag, seemingly dazed by recent events, shook her head.

"Heather," she said. "You are a profound idiot."

Magenta marched on, grinning with satisfaction. The Gods were obviously with her. And she had every right to expect that they would be, for she was assiduously consulting Zeus, Apollo and Athena at every opportunity, and she always followed their advice.

Only yesterday she had lost the poppy to the young hippie girl. Shaken by this defeat, Magenta had sat down to consult an oracle, the insides of a dead pigeon. A commotion in the sky made her look up, and there was a battle between various Persian winged demons.

Cyrus might be dead, but she was not returning home without profit. The triple-bloomed Welsh poppy and a small and gleaning octagonal mirror had plummeted down into her lap from the sky. Recognizing valuable booty when she saw it, Xenophon gathered them up and hurried off.

"Well, I wasn't to know you were involved in some shady dealing on behalf of that dumb woman Kerry," protested Heather. "I thought you were being mugged."

Heather was indignant. She had risked her life to save a fellow Scot from the enemy and all she got was abuse.

"Now we don't have the mirror anymore and neither do we have the flower. You have ruined everything. Why do you have to leap into everything feet first? Or sword first?"

"We MacKintoshes are used to fighting," replied Heather, stiffly. "Remember, we had to hold off the filthy Camerons for generations."

"I thought it was the MacPhersons," said Dinnie.

"We had a feud with the Camerons as well. A desperate affair, though not as bad as the one we had with the disgusting Comyns. Now that was a feud. Bloody deaths everywhere."

Dinnie shook his head in despair. Morag departed in disgust.

"To hell with it," sneered Heather. "Last time I risk my life for her. Still, I am interested to learn that Kerry wants to win the East Fourth Community Arts Prize. That piece of information is bound to prove useful to us."

She returned to the subject of Dinnie's diet.

"For the meantime you will have to make do without the Chinese cabbage leaves."

"What? You expect me to eat these nuts on their own? You promised me green vegetables."

"Well you can hardly expect me to come back with an armful of Chinese cabbage leaves when the entire market was filled with yellow fairies hacking at me with curved swords and axes, can you? You'll just have to make do. Now excuse me, I am off for a well-earned dram."

FOURTEEN

"Surely it can be repaired?"
"No, it can't."

Morag was lying facedown on a cushion, her head resting heavily on a cassette of L7's new album. In normal times she liked the way these women screamed and hit their guitars, but now she was in the depths of incurable depression. Her rescue mission had gone disastrously wrong and her fiddle was still in ruins.

"This fiddle is the product of Callum MacHardie and he is the finest fiddle maker in Scotland. The MacHardies, fairies and humans, have always made the best fiddles. This one took Callum three years to make and another year's wait before varnishing. It's made of maple and pine and ebony and boxwood, and the amber varnish Callum uses is a secret only he knows. Now it's in bits. I don't even know if Callum himself could fix it if he had it in his workshop under the Sacred Ash Tree. Who could repair it here?"

"New York must have skilled violin makers."

"Would they work on a fiddle four inches long?"

Kerry sprawled on the cushion beside Morag. Her most precious flower was missing. It could not be replaced. After Morag fell from the sky during the fiasco with the Chinese fairies, the original had again disappeared, and she had already scoured the wasteland where it had grown. There was nothing else there like it."

Kerry played a listless version of the New York Dolls' "Lonely Planet Boy," but without Morag playing along it didn't feel the same and they soon lapsed into listening to gloomy Swans records instead.

There were three weeks left before the closing date for entries to the Arts competition. Kerry, who would have had her work cut out gathering the remaining flowers even without the recent setbacks, seemed to be defeated. Cal and his version of *A Midsummer Night's Dream* seemed destined to win the prize, no matter how terrible his version might turn out to be. The only other entrants Kerry knew of were poets, and poets were not fashionable right now.

Unexpectedly, Heather flew in the window. She felt that some sort of apology was in order and, having drunk enough whisky, had come to make it. She said she was sorry about the mix-up and volunteered to do all she could to help rectify the situation.

In this she was quite sincere, although it was at the back of her mind that the more she knew about Kerry's flower alphabet the more likely it was that she could make something out of it to benefit Dinnie. She was careful to give no hint of this, knowing that Morag would be irate at the thought of a match between her pleasant friend and the unlovely Dinnie.

It was a beautiful day in Cornwall, the sort of day when fairies should be out playing music and sniffing flowers. Most of them were toiling in workhouses, however, and the few that weren't were hiding in a barn, plotting revolution.

"So, Aelric, what's the next step?"

"Further economic disruption," said Aelric.

"But there are not enough of us to ruin the King's economy

as you say we must."

Aelric admitted that this was true and told them the next stage was to spread the revolt.

"A peasants' revolution is what we need, although how we manage this, I am not sure. From the subject index in the library, Chairman Mao seems to be the acknowledged expert on the subject, but there are an awful lot of books by him and I haven't quite mastered his tactics yet."

They all prayed to Dianna, Goddess of the Fairies, for help because it would have been quite shocking for them not to, even if, as Aelric had discovered, Chairman Mao had decidedly strong views against this sort of thing.

Morag sat with Heather on the fire escape outside Dinnie's.

"Don't worry," Heather comforted her. "Your hair is looking beautiful with all its colors and the beads Kerry gave you suit you really well. And when we get back to Scotland you can get a new fiddle. You are such a great player that Callum MacHardie will be happy to make you a bonnie new one, even if he does disapprove of you playing Ramones tunes on it. And in the meantime, you can share mine."

Morag's spirits rose slightly. It was good to at least be friends with Heather again.

"Having a nice rest?" came Dinnie's voice from behind.

Dinnie was scowling. Something he would not admit even to himself was that he was jealous of the relationship between Heather and Morag. He did not wish them to be friends again in case Heather left him alone.

"You're meant to be giving me a violin lesson."

"Hold your wheesht," said Heather, brusquely.

"What?"

"Be quiet."

"Oh, fine," said Dinnie. "Abuse me. I don't remember that

being part of our bargain."

"What bargain?" asked Morag.

"Nothing, nothing," chirped Heather.

They began to talk together in Gaelic, which made Dinnie more frustrated. A pleasantly malicious thought entered his head. He could think of one very easy way to get rid of Morag and put one over on Heather, whom he still resented for making him diet.

"When you've quite finished, Heather, could you get on with teaching me how to play my fine MacPherson fiddle?"

There was a brief silence.

"Fine what?" said Morag.

Heather paled slightly.

"Nothing, nothing."

"He said fine MacPherson fiddle," stated Morag. "And I am beginning to have one of those psychic insights which . . ."

She sped across the room and climbed right onto the instrument to study it. Heather placed her tiny hand across her brow and rested her head against the filthy cooker. She knew what was coming.

Morag shrieked with delight.

"It's the MacPherson fiddle! The real MacPherson fiddle. You found it!"

She danced around happily.

"What a wonderful coincidence. The treasure of my clan, right here on East Fourth Street. And the only fiddle I would rather play than my own! Everything is turning out well. Heather, help me shrink it to our size so I can play!"

"She will do no such thing," declared Dinnie smugly. "It's mine until I hand it over to Heather. That's our bargain. So beat it."

"What does he mean?" asked Morag. "It obviously should be mine. I'm a MacPherson."

"She has a bargain with me," repeated Dinnie, "which cannot be broken."

"Is this true?"

"Well . . ." said Heather, who could neither deny nor break the bargain.

"But my fiddle is broken. I need it."

"Tough," said Dinnie, who was enjoying himself greatly.

Morag erupted into a terrible fury. Heather had never seen her in such a state. Morag claimed the fiddle as hers by right of being a MacPherson and called Heather a thief, a cheat and a liar.

Dinnie chuckled to himself. He had known very well what would happen if Morag found out about the bargain.

"I can't help it," protested Heather. "I made the bargain with the human and a good thistle fairy is not allowed to break a bargain."

Morag's pale skin was scarlet with rage.

"The violin belongs to my clan, you lizard."

"Please, Morag . . ."

"And you are a goblin fucker and a disgrace to Scotland."

This was too much, even for a contrite Heather.

"Well, you ignorant MacPhersons shouldn't have lost it in the first place."

"You MacKintoshes are all scum," yelled Morag. "I spit in your mother's milk!"

With this approximation of an insult she'd picked up in a Mexican restaurant, Morag stormed out the window.

Heather hung her head. What a disaster. Thank the Goddess Morag had not thought to ask what the other half of the bargain was. If she discovered that Heather was intending to pair off Dinnie and Kerry, things might have gotten violent.

"Dear, dear," said Dinnie. "What a terrible argument. How tactless of me."

Heather gave him a ferocious glower but did not argue.

"Next lesson. Holding the bow. And this time try not to saw the damn thing in half."

FIFTEEN

Everywhere there were dissatisfied fairies. While Heather and Morag had their own various problems, they had caused problems for others as well.

"Where does this money come from?" asked both Dinnie and Kerry, noticing that both Heather and Morag liked to keep the houses well stocked with provisions.

"Standard fairy magic," lied Heather and Morag.

But on Grand Street the Italian fairies were most unhappy. Unknown strangers kept robbing their human allies' banks.

"Four times this month," they grumbled. "We cannot let our Italian friends' businesses be ruined by these thieves."

On Canal Street the Chinese fairies were still fuming over the theft of their Bhat Gwa mirror. This important icon had been given to the Chinese fairies two thousand years ago by the blessed Lao Tzu before he departed the Earth. It was their greatest treasure and was housed in the shop of Hwui-Yin as a symbol of friendship between fairies and humans.

Now, on the verge of seeing it returned, they had been frustrated by another unknown fairy who had brandished a sword at them and screamed abuse in a horrible barbaric accent.

"We are a peaceable tribe. But we cannot tolerate this."

They wondered who was responsible. It could be the Italian fairies, whom they had known in the past but had no contact with now, even though they lived only a few blocks away.

In Harlem there was a great upset over the incident at the bar. It was most impolite for strangers to come and rob a place in their territory and the violent threats from the red-haired stranger caused great concern.

"We have not seen any other fairies here for generations," they said. "And now they come like thieves. We must prepare for the worst."

In Central Park, Brannoc was extremely dissatisfied. He had just found Tulip and Petal making love enthusiastically under a rose bush. It was not taboo for a fairy brother and sister to have sex, but it annoyed the hell out of Brannoc. He burned with jealousy.

Maeve and Padraig were drunk and maudlin. They sat in a tree playing their tin whistles. Brannoc had to admit he was impressed at the way these Irish musicians could still play so well after drinking so much, but he was not in the mood to be appreciative.

Petal and Tulip were nowhere in sight. Presumably they were still practicing their youthful fairy sex techniques, although from what Brannoc had seen they seemed fairly advanced already.

Brannoc felt lonely. It struck him that only a little way to the north were a whole new tribe of fairies he could be friendly with. If he was to go back he was sure he could make good the argument. He was a reasonable fairy. He saw no reason why they should not be. It was not good to make enemies in this strange place.

"Where are you going," called Padraig.

"To make peace with the black fairies," he replied.

"Good luck. Bring us some whisky."

In Cornwall also there was great dissatisfaction. The fairies of the land were no longer allowed to pay tribute to their Goddess Dianna. Her festivals had been replaced by ceremonies dedicated to a strong new god who would defeat their enemies.

The moon appeared from behind the clouds. Magris spoke a few more words of the old tongue and a moonbow in seven shades of grey slid out of the sky.

Half of the mercenary band climbed the moonbow and made their way up into the night. They climbed without a sound till they disappeared from view. Magris returned and muttered to the remaining mercenaries. They marched off into the night on the track of the rebel Aelric.

The light wind that always followed the production of a moonbow tugged at Magris's cloak as he too left.

Magenta was tense, though not dissatisfied. She eyed the skyscrapers that stretched up First Avenue and her soldierly instinct told her that here would be a good place for an ambush. Joshua, now merged in her mind with Tissaphernes, might be waiting round any corner. She took a drink from her cocktail, made a mental note to buy more methylated spirits and boot polish, and flicked through her copy of Xenophon.

One of the most impressive parts of the book was the Greek's trust in the Gods. Even in the most dangerous circumstances, when quick action was imperative, they would do nothing until they had made the proper sacrifices and consulted the omens.

Magenta looked around for a likely sacrifice. A squashed pigeon lay in the gutter. Magenta spied it and hurried over to inspect its entrails. They were a little hard to read, having been run over by numerous cars, but on the whole Magenta thought they looked favorable.

"Right, men," she called. "Advance."

There were more dissatisfied fairies in Cornwall. In a corner of Bodmin Moor behind an ancient standing stone, a corner as grey and cold as the Atlantic over which the mercenaries strode, the moonbow was about to fade in the dawn. Out of the bush crept four silent figures, scanning the area warily.

"Where is it leading," whispered one, eyeing the seven bands of grey.

"Who knows?" said another. "But Heather MacKintosh and Morag MacPherson will be on the end of it. Let us go before it fades."

Without another word they began to ascend. They were four female warrior fairies from the MacLeod clan. Each of them was tall, lithe and strong, and heavily armed. They intended to recover the stolen piece of their banner and none of them had the manner of one to be trifled with.

A small child dropped a dime on the sidewalk. Brannoc kindly stopped to pick it up and return it.

"I don't believe it," came a voice. "Not content with robbing the bars, they're stealing dimes off children now."

Brannoc was confronted by an angry group of black fairies.

"These whites are even meaner than they used to be."

"You don't understand," protested Brannoc.

"Someone's stolen my dime," wailed the child.

Brannoc made a hurried departure, learning with great speed the technique, already well known to Heather and Morag, of making an emergency exit on the fender of a speeding cab.

"What happened?" cried Tulip and Petal as he stumbled into the safety of their bushes. Brannoc refused to talk about it, although he did mention that cab drivers in New York were appallingly reckless, luckily for him.

SIXTEEN

"I saw an awful lot of police outside," said Morag, as Kerry took her lunchtime steroids.

Kerry told her that they were probably on their way to Tompkins Square, where today there was a free festival.

"I hate to see so many police."

"Why?" enquired Morag. "Police are nice. In Cruickshank our village police man, Constable MacBain, is a braw man. Every afternoon after he has his dinner and a few drinks at the pub he comes for a sleep behind the bushes where we live and he often leaves some tobacco for the fairies. All the children like him because he gives them rides on his bicycle. And he is not a bad piper, either. Now I think about it, I'm sure I heard him say one day that he has an Irish cousin who is a policeman in America. I'm sure he is a braw man too."

Kerry said that this did not sound like any policeman she had ever come across, and chances of any number of the New York Police department leaving tobacco out for the fairies were pretty slim, but Morag did not really understand what she meant.

"So, what are we going to do today?"

"The festival in Tompkins Square. Cal is playing guitar with a friend's band so we can scream abuse."

"Sounds good to me."

Kerry struggled into her pink and green dungarees because today she would need lots of pockets for beer. After a long and detailed discussion with Morag about what to pin in their hair, involving much study of Botticelli's *Primavera* and associated works, they left.

In Chinatown the Chinese fairies were making final preparations for the Festival of Hungry Ghosts, making sure they had enough food and drink for celebration and for offerings, and the correct incense and paper money for burning. This active time would normally have been a happy one, but the community was instead gripped with apprehension due to the loss of their prized Bhat Gwa mirror. What new and terrible dissatisfied spirit might appear among them without the mirror to reflect away bad Fung Shui?

Lu-Tang, their sage and wise woman, sent envoys all over looking for it, but where it had got to since last seen falling from the skies onto Canal Street, no one could tell.

Further inspections of Kerry's apartment showed that it was no longer there, although the Chinese fairies who staked out East Fourth Street were interested to see Heather sneak into the apartment for a good look around.

Heather was taking this opportunity to break into Kerry's apartment and gather more information about her. The more she knew about Kerry's tastes, the easier it would be to change Dinnie into the sort of person she would like.

She wondered where they had gone.

"To have fun somewhere, no doubt," she muttered wistfully, rummaging through Kerry's huge collection of cassettes, and wishing again that she had ended up with a human friend who liked to have fun, instead of one who sat around all day watching dubious programs on the television.

It took Kerry some time to persuade Morag that they had not actually been responsible for the riot in Tompkins Square and that it was merely a coincidence that it had erupted after they lobbed a bottle onstage at Cal's band.

"I'm sure there would have been trouble anyway," proclaimed Kerry, as they fled from the chaos. "It had little or nothing to do with us drinking too much. The police were just waiting for an opportunity to wade in with their truncheons."

Bloodied victims of the riot streamed past them, much to Morag's distress.

"The police here are very heavy-handed," she said, wincing at the sight of the injuries. "I will have some strong words to say to Constable MacBain when I get back to Scotland."

As soon as they were out of the immediate area they plunged into a deli to buy a beer.

"Why do they sell beer in brown bags here," enquired Morag.

"Something to do with the law."

"Oh. I thought it made it taste better. Still, we'd better obey the law unless we want to get a truncheon over the head."

Magenta hurried past on the other side of the street, escaping after the vicious melee with the Persians. Morag spotted her and gave pursuit.

"Well," mused Johnny Thunders, gently floating down through the Nether Worlds. "I can hear screaming guitars and a riot going on. Sounds like New York to me."

He was right. It was.

"Now, how am I to find my 1958 Gibson Tiger Top?"

In the mad pursuit into the mountainous regions Magenta, badly harassed by Persian mounted archers, New York motor-cycle police and a Scottish fairy, was forced to abandon some of the booty picked up on the campaign so far.

This was regrettable because, as with all mercenaries, booty was one of her main motivations. Mercenary pay was not really sufficient to justify the dangers and rigors of the life. However, they were too heavily laden and something had to go. She dropped the triple-bloomed Welsh poppy and carried on with her flight.

She was protecting the rear. Up in the front Christophus the Spartan led the way. Xenophon did not trust Christophus one bit.

"The bag lady is madder than the rest of them," Morag told Kerry. "Younger and fitter, though. It took me fourteen blocks to catch up with her."

"What happened?"

"I asked her for the flower. She shouted at some imaginary followers to form a square because they were under attack. Then she threw down the poppy."

"Did you get it?"

Morag shook her head.

"Three fire trucks arrived at that very minute. By the time I'd made my way around them it was gone."

She gazed at her knee, which was red.

"When I tried running around the fire trucks I fell over and skinned my knee. I think the beer may have slightly affected my balance.

Kerry trudged home with Morag in her pocket. She needed this flower and it was high time it stopped circulating round the city, but who could say where it was now?

SEVENTEEN

"Your waistline is definitely getting smaller," announced Heather. "Have you done your exercises today?"

Dinnie nodded. He had never exercised before and he ached.

"Good. Soon you will be a fine strapping MacKintosh, fit for anything. Now, who do you like best, the Velvet Underground or Sonic Youth?"

Dinnie shook his head blankly, one of the many habits of his which annoyed the fairy.

"The Velvet Underground? Sonic Youth? What are you talking about?"

"I have made an important discovery."

"You have to leave?"

"No, I don't have to leave. To fulfill our bargain, I am prepared to hang around indefinitely. The important discovery I made, during a daring commando raid on Kerry's, is that she is very fond of music. There are these things—what are they called—cassettes? Right? Cassettes. All over the place. She is almost as untidy as you, though not so dirty. Now, of course I had not heard of any of the bands that played on these cassettes, but I picked out the one she plays most often—"

"And how did you find that out?" said Dinnie, with some sarcasm. "Asked a cockroach, I suppose?"

"No, I did not ask a cockroach. I asked the cassettes."

Heather picked something out of her sporran.

"And here it is."

Dinnie glared woefully at the tape. "A New York Compilation," it was called: Sonic Youth, the Ramones, the New York Dolls, Lydia Lunch, Richard Hell, the Swans, Nine Inch Nails, Television and many others.

"Well, so what?"

Heather scowled in frustration.

"Dinnie, stop havering. If you want to be the sort of boyfriend Kerry will like you will have to at least pretend to like the same sort of music as her. Haven't you seen her going out to hear bands at night? It is obviously important to her."

Dinnie was appalled.

"Is there no end to these impositions?" he barked. Only yesterday Heather had lectured him for refusing to give money to a beggar and right after that she had forbidden him to call the assistant at the deli a Mexican whore, even in private.

"This is not the sort of thing Kerry will want to hear. And you are not to mutter bad things under your breath when black people come on the television either."

Heather waved aside his protests and inserted the cassette in Dinnie's tape recorder. "Now you listen to this and memorize it. I am away for a few drams and I'll test you when I get back."

Dinnie, however, had not finished protesting.

"What use will it be liking the same sort of music as her when I'll probably never even get the chance to talk to her?"

Heather slapped her thigh triumphantly.

"I was hoping you'd ask that. Because I have that angle covered as well. When you make a bargain with a MacKintosh fairy you get full service."

"Kerry, as I have told you, is very fond of flowers. She seems to collect them, in dried form at least. And today, while having my afternoon flutter along the rooftops, I happened to spot a very unusual flower lying on the pavement."

She handed the triple-bloomed poppy to Dinnie.

"I feel that once you give this to her she will be very favorably disposed towards you."

Heather stood on the play button of Dinnie's cassette deck.

Dinnie winced as Lydia Lunch began to play though his rooms.

"But I hate this sort of stuff."

"So what? You can pretend. You don't think you're going to win Kerry by being sincere, do you?"

Aelric's guerrilla campaign in Cornwall suffered a reverse when he fell in love with the King's stepdaughter.

He sat in a barn, musing on his misfortune.

"Are you sure you are in love with her?" asked Aelis, one of his trusted companions.

"Yes. When I saw her drawing her sword and preparing to give chase after we set fire to Tala's royal mint, I knew immediately."

Aelis shook her head in sympathy. She knew that when a fairy falls in love at first sight it is practically impossible to get over it, but she also knew that as a romance it was doomed from the start. With Marion being the stepdaughter of the King there seemed little chance of her falling for Aelric, a rebel who kept burning down the King's most important buildings.

Barn owls nestled in the shade beside them.

Aelric looked thoughtfully at the ceiling.

"Of course," he mused, "she is his stepdaughter and for all I know she might hate her father. Stepdaughters have a notoriously bad time of it in fairy royal families."

Aelis agreed that this was possible and promised to find out from one of her contacts, a handmaiden at the royal palace, the precise standing of the King's stepdaughter.

The rest of the guerrilla unit stole silently into the barn in preparation for the night's raid.

On the problem of how Morag was to obtain the MacPherson fiddle from Dinnie, Kerry had a useful suggestion.

"Offer Dinnie something better than Heather has. Then he would give you the fiddle."

Morag considered it. It seemed like a good idea.

"Except I don't know what that scumbag of a MacKintosh has offered," complained the fairy and spat on the floor.

"In that case you will have to offer him what he wants most in all the world. And as he seems like a lonely soul, I imagine what he would most like is a nice girlfriend. Unless he is gay, in which case he would like a nice boyfriend."

Morag fluttered across the road.

"Dinnie," she asked. "Are you gay or straight?"

"How dare you!" roared Dinnie, and threw a cup at her.

She fluttered back.

"That probably means he is straight, though somewhat prejudiced," explained Kerry.

"Then I will bargain with him for a girlfriend," declared Morag. "Although finding anyone who would want to go out with that abusive lump will be a sore test."

Heather stared sadly at the corpse in the doorway. Two policemen were attending to it.

"I can't understand why these tramps keep dying on East Fourth," said one, and the other shook his head. This made eight in the past two weeks.

"Call Linda at 970 F-U-C-K for the hottest two-girl sex in town."

Dinnie was watching television.

"I presume you are now fully expert in New York music?" said Heather, appearing in the sudden way which was so distressing to Dinnie. She switched off the TV and worked the cassette.

"Who's this?"

"The Velvet Underground."

"Wrong. It's the Ramones. What about this one?"

"Band of Susans."

"Wrong. It is Suicide. You have failed. Listen to the tape again. I am going to sleep, but do not worry about disturbing me. I am becoming fonder of that funny sweet American whisky and I am now able to drink more of it."

"You mean you're drunk."

"Drunk? Me? A MacKintosh fairy?" Heather laughed and slumped on the bed.

Kerry was enormously depressed about everything. Her flower alphabet, while growing steadily, was missing its most important component. Her disease did not seem to be getting any better, which made her drink more, which made her more depressed afterward. And seeing Cal on stage with his band had been a sore trial.

Kerry wished that he had stayed with her and carried out his promise to teach her all the New York Dolls guitar solos.

"I miss Cal," she told Morag. "And even throwing a bottle at him and ruining his gig has not driven him out of my mind."

"Find a new man," suggested Morag. "While I am finding a new woman for Dinnie."

Kerry said that this was not so easy.

Morag stared at the adverts on the back of *Village Voice*.

"Transvestites, Singles, Bi's, Gays, all welcome, Club Eidelweiss, West Twenty-Ninth St."

"Young man on Brooklyn-bound 'B' train, Thursday 6/21, light jeans, got off at Dekalb Ave, I was too shy to talk, would like to hear from you."

"I see that it can be difficult to make relationships here."

When Dinnie once more failed to identify any of the bands correctly, both he and Heather were frustrated. Dinnie had come around to agreeing that it was a good idea, but he could not manage a single right answer.

"They all sound the same to me. I'll never be able to tell Cop Shoot Cop from the Swans. Kerry will never fall in love with me."

Heather pursed her lips. This was proving more difficult than she had imagined.

She fingered her kilt. Back in Scotland Heather had ripped it deliberately to outrage her mother, but now, after so much traveling, it was in danger of disintegrating completely. She took out her dirk, and cut a little piece from one of Dinnie's cushion covers to make a bright patch. Perhaps while sewing she would find some inspiration. If she had known what Morag across the street was thinking she would have agreed. This city was a difficult place to make relationships. The way things were going, Dinnie might as well call up 970 C-U-N-T and get on with it.

Still, she thought, there was always the flower. The poppy with its three blooms seemed like a very special sort of flower. She was sure that once Dinnie presented it to Kerry she would look on him favorably.

EIGHTEEN

It rained—a strange warm rain that was unfamiliar to Morag. In Scotland the rain had been cold, cheerless and grey. This warm summer rain disquieted her, though she could not say why.

"Kerry, I have just had a good idea."

"Yes?"

"About Dinnie and the fiddle. The idea that he might swap it for love is very sound. However, what are the chances of any woman falling in love with him?"

Slim, they both agreed.

"So," continued Morag. "I will be unable to make a true bargain with him. There is only one thing to do."

"What?"

"Be deceitful."

"You mean lie?"

"Not exactly. If I were able to lie to humans I could simply steal the fiddle, but if I did that, terrible things would follow. As you have already observed, fairy karma is a bitch. Me and my clan might be cursed for generations.

"So I will merely bend the truth a little. Bending the truth a little is a respectable fairy tradition.

"I will gain the instrument and return to Scotland in triumph. I will be forgiven everything. My clan will no longer shun me for playing Ramones riffs on my fiddle. The MacLeods will not bother me anymore as I will be a Scottish hero. Quite possibly I will be made sole recipient of the junior fiddling prize. Evil MacKintosh objections will wither away in the face of such a mighty feat. Yes, I am sure that deceit is the best way forward."

"So what do you plan to do?"

"I will pretend to Dinnie that I could convince you to be his girlfriend. He is bound to go for it. You would be a girlfriend away and beyond his wildest dreams. Whatever that raghead Heather has offered will look paltry by comparison. All it will require is for you to lead him on a little. Once I have the fiddle, you can tell him to go boil his head."

Dinnie, in addition to listening to rock music, was under standing instructions to keep an eye on the street below in case Kerry appeared. Once she did he was to hurry down and present her with the Welsh poppy.

"It will be an excellent introduction," Heather assured him.

Unfortunately when Kerry did appear in the street, hurrying between her apartment and the deli for some beer, Dinnie's nerve failed him and she returned home before he could work up the nerve to accost her.

"You fat useless lump," said Heather, and roundly criticized him as a disgrace to the fighting MacKintoshes.

"Give me the flower!" she said, seeing that she would have to start the process herself. "I will take it to her and tell her it is a present from you. Now I think about it, this will be even better. Any young woman receiving a present of a flower from a fairy can hardly fail to be impressed. She will fall into your arms."

This decided, she placed the poppy in her bag, slung it over her shoulder and departed, promising as she did to bring some money home for rent.

Back in Cornwall, Aelis had some bad news for Aelric.

Marion, the King's stepdaughter, apparently got on unusually well with Tala, and also with her mother. They were a notably happy family.

"How depressing," said Aelric. "And Tala such a monster as well. Still, I remember seeing in the library that Hitler was a good family man so perhaps it is not so surprising. It just goes to show that step-parents get bad press. What am I going to do now? I have twelve followers, not nearly enough to disrupt the Cornish fairy economy, and a hopeless passion for the King's stepdaughter."

Aelis took a swig of mead from her flask and considered the matter.

"Well, Aelric, you must find some way to win her heart. Of course, burning down her father's property will always put a bit of a damper on the relationship, but maybe something will turn up. My contact at the court tells me she is very fond of flowers so perhaps you could do something in that direction. As for recruiting more followers, we must get on with distributing our propaganda leaflets.

This, while a good idea, was proving to be a problem. With the strongest flyers from Tala's army guarding the airspace above all his most vital institutions and population centers, the rebels had been unable to distribute a single one.

Heather's day had started off well after a few drams and a visit to the West Village to look around the expensive art galleries and shops. After that it had gone seriously downhill. She now hung on grimly to the rear mud-guard of a speeding motorbike as it thundered round the corner at Delancey and Allen. Behind her, twenty Italian fairies hung on to the roof of a wailing ambulance in hot pursuit.

"What sort of a motorbike courier are you?" she yelled furiously as the bike stopped at an intersection. "Jump the lights!"

Behind her the ambulance had also halted, but the Italian fairies, using their unusual affinity with the wind currents, swept forward through the air from one vehicle to the next. When the lights changed and Heather's bike took off they were no more than four vehicles behind.

Heather had robbed the Bank d'Italia one time too many. They had been waiting for her outside and she had been caught red-handed with a sporran full of dollars.

Racing up Allen Street and over Houston, Heather began to despair. The Italian fairies had transferred themselves onto a fire truck and were going fast.

At the last moment, as the fire truck drew level and her pursuers prepared to leap across, Heather, in desperation, jumped blindly out into Second Street. She was then extremely fortunate. A small and fast foreign sports car, which at that moment was being pursued by the police, screeched by and she caught hold of the aerial. The car carried her along Second Street and into Avenue A while her pursuers, taken by surprise, disappeared from view on the fire truck.

Heather's car was brought to a halt by police gunfire at the end of Fourth Street and she slipped off to hurry home.

Morag was out for some air and saw her frantic arrival.

"What on earth have you been doing?" she said. "Why are the police shooting at you?"

"They're not shooting at me, you idiot," exclaimed Heather. "Oh no!"

The Italian fairies reappeared, cruising their way along on a Ford with music blasting out of the huge speakers built into the rear of the chassis.

"Get her!" they screamed.

The two Scottish fairies leapt onto a cab and fled.

The moonbow stretched from Cornwall to Manhattan and on it marched the mercenaries. At their head was Werferth, a ferocious Red Cap from the Northern borders of England. Behind him marched three red-haired Pechs from Scotland and at their sides trotted three Cu Sidth dogs with green fur and malevolent eyes.

The company contained more of the frightening border Red Caps along with Bwabachods from Wales, Spriggans from Cornwall and various other fierce creatures. They had gold in their pockets, a half-payment from Magris, and they did not anticipate any difficulty in earning the rest. The moonbow bent and warped space and distance, making the journey between Britain and America no more than a day's march. America was now in sight and they quickened their pace.

"Well, if you continually rob banks you have to expect this sort of thing!" whispered Morag.

They were hiding on a fire escape, at the bottom of Orchard Street.

"Maybe," whispered Heather. "But I swear that when they were screaming abuse at me from the fire truck they said something about being continually plundered by *two* fairies in kilts."

"Was that a firecracker?" muttered Morag. "I did not quite see which way the cab took us. Are we anywhere near Chinatown?"

There was a sudden shout from above.

"It's them!"

They looked up and groaned. Swarming down the fire escape was an army of Chinese fairies, yelling in triumph.

Some way behind the mercenaries, the warriors from the MacLeod clan strode easily over the moonbow. They were clad in dark leather tunics and their kilts were green with stripes of yellow and red.

The four sisters; their names were Ailsa, Seónaid, Mairi and Rhona and their home was on the banks of Loch Dunvegan in the west of the Isle of Skye. They lived in sight of Dunvegan Castle, ancestral home of the MacLeods of MacLeod, leaders of the human branch of the clan.

The MacLeods had fought many fierce battles in the distant past. There had been a time when the human MacLeods had waged continual war on the MacDonalds of Eigg, their hereditary enemies, and the MacLeod fairies had done likewise with the MacDonald fairies.

The MacLeod fairies and humans had been closely allied since the far distant time when Malcolm MacLeod, chief of the human clan, married a shape-changing fairy wife. They had a son before she went back to her own folk, and the legendary MacLeod fairy banner was a gift to the son. It was a thing of great power and could never be unfurled except in times of dire need.

On one occasion during battle with the MacDonalds, the MacLeods were on the point of defeat. Their chief unfurled the green Fairy Banner and immediately the fairies came to his aid and won the day. For Heather and Morag to cut two pieces from it was the most sacrilegious thing they could possibly have done. It was no surprise that the MacLeods had sent their most feared fighters to regain the pieces.

"This is as bad as the time the MacLeods chased us from Loch Morar to Loch Ness," groaned Morag.

"It sure is," agreed Heather and winced at the memory.

After an extremely long chase they had been on the very point of capture when they fortunately ran into a group of MacAndrew fairies. As the MacAndrews were associates of the MacKintoshes they had been willing to protect Heather and also her companion, enabling them to escape.

Later, though, there had been no protection anywhere from the powerful MacLeods and their allies. Heather and Morag's clans could not go to war on their behalf when they were so obviously in the wrong.

Now they sat atop another fire truck which was racing north, sirens wailing.

Behind them the Chinese fairies were pursuing on motor cars.

"Lucky for us there's lots of fires in New York."

Heather declared that she was definitely innocent of angering the Chinese fairies and demanded to know what Morag had been doing to them.

"Nothing. I only freed a few lobsters. And it wasn't me that stole their brooch, I was just an accessory after the fact. Obviously these New York fairies have no manners."

Heather nodded.

"You're right there. I mean, what's wrong with taking dollars from a bank to buy food? Nothing to get upset about. There's millions of spare dollars in that bank. Nobody will miss a few. If everybody took some then there wouldn't be all those poor people begging on the streets."

They seemed to be outdistancing their pursuers.

"We're losing them."

The fire truck came to a halt outside a burning apartment building. The two Scots jumped down. Another fire truck roared up alongside. Seemingly hanging off every available handhold were white-clad Italian fairies.

Heather and Morag fled.

Ailsa was the oldest MacLeod sister and the leader. They were descended from Gara, the original fairy who married the human chief, and all four of them were hardened warriors. They had high cheekbones, large dark eyes and jagged black hair cut short. Their claymores were keen and hung over their backs and the sharpened dirks strapped to their legs had been handed down through generations of warriors.

"When we find the MacPherson and the MacKintosh, are we to kill them?" asked Mairi.

"If need be," replied Ailsa. "Although I have a sleep spell with me. We will try that first. How much farther have we to go, Mairi?"

Mairi had the second sight.

"Not much farther. I can sense a very strange land only a little way away."

"Where are we?"

Heather shrugged. Neither she nor Morag had been this far north before.

"Have we shaken them off?"

"I think so."

"How are we ever going to get back to Fourth Street?"

The cab had sped all the way up to East 106th before turning left. Heather and Morag dismounted on Fifth Avenue and looked around them.

"That was a long journey. And we're still in the city. What a massive place."

"Look! There is some countryside."

In front of them Central Park was green and appealing.

"At least we can rest for a while."

"We've found the thieves!" yelled the leader of a hunting party from the black fairies. "After them."

The mercenaries were over Manhattan. Werferth halted the company and they stared down at the alien land. It was dusk but the city was lit up brighter than anything they had seen before. The huge array of human buildings was off-putting, but the moonbow stretched down into what appeared to be a large wooded field.

"Right, lads," said Werferth. "Down we go."

They began their descent into the foreign land.

"I absolutely did not do anything to offend any black fairies," said Morag, perched on the back of a mountain bike. "I never even met a black fairy before."

"Me neither," said Heather. "They are obviously paranoid about strangers."

The bicycle raced around the north edge of the park.

"Lucky for us this cyclist has good powerful legs."

Heather and Morag flew from the bicycle onto a passing horse and carriage carrying tourists, and from there made their way to Broadway via a busking juggler riding a unicycle.

"This way," yelled Morag, and leapt onto a car going south.

The car took them steadily down Broadway.

"I think we've finally shaken everybody off."

They began to relax a little. They were now near Union Square, far away from the black fairies.

A stretch limo drew up alongside them. On top of it, to Heather and Morag's horrified amazement, were four figures from their nightmares. Brandishing claymores and preparing to board their car were the dreaded MacLeod sisters.

NINETEEN

Kerry lay on the floor drawing her comic. This was one of the numerous artistic enterprises she carried out mainly for her own amusement. The comic was causing her problems. Inspired by Morag and Heather it was meant to be about fairies, but as Kerry mainly liked to write about fairies, or people, being kind to one another, it was short on action. Morag hobbled painfully into the room.

"Morag? What's wrong?"

The fairy slumped onto a yellow cushion. She was so stiff and sore she could barely move.

Kerry did her best to make a good cup of tea. Morag loved tea but Kerry, along with the rest of New York, was lamentable at making it.

Morag told Kerry about the day's terrible events: her pursuit by the Italians, Chinese, black fairies, and finally the MacLeods.

"How did you escape?"

"We leapt off the car and started running when suddenly we were scooped up by a person who hid us in her shopping bag. Some time later when we poked our heads out the MacLeods were nowhere in sight. Strangely enough, our rescuer was none other than the funny lady who had your Welsh poppy.

"She told us not to worry because she had rescued us from

Carduchan tribesmen, whoever they are, and to remember that Xenophon was the best leader of the army, in case it ever came to a vote between her and Christophus the Spartan. What this means, I am unclear."

Morag hung her head a little.

"Unfortunately she then took the poppy again."

"What? Where from?"

"From Heather. She was bringing it for you from Dinnie."

"How did Dinnie get it?"

Morag shrugged.

"Anyway, the stupid wee midden took it out of her sporran and started waving it about. The bag lady said that it was not fitting for mere Pelasts to be in charge of so much valuable booty and claimed it was hers by right of conquest."

Kerry was aghast.

"It certainly gets around, this flower."

"Oh, well," said Kerry. "At least you escaped."

"Well, sort of. Except we were just turning onto East Fourth Street when I remarked to Heather that if any of the Italian fairies were like me, that is, well known for psychic insights, they might well be waiting for us. They were. They took the money back. What a terrible day. I ache all over. My Indian headband is ruined. Have we got any whisky?"

Morag sipped her drink.

"It was nice seeing Heather, though. Till we argued."

"'Tullochgorum' again?"

Morag shook her head.

"Not at first. She accused me of deliberately putting my feet in her face in Magenta's shopping bag. Stupid besom. I was only trying to get comfy. Then she said no wonder the MacPhersons couldn't play strathspeys properly if they all had such big feet to worry about. Completely uncalled for. After that we argued about 'Tullochgorum.' Then the incident with the poppy happened and I threatened to kill her for losing your flower. It really was a terrible day."

Magenta trundled on. She was satisfied with the day's events. She had rescued her men from a serious attack and begged enough money to replenish her cocktail. Best of all, she had regained her booty. The Welsh poppy was now dear to her heart, as dear as the guitar fragments she carried in her shopping bag, and she would fight to the death to keep hold of it.

Kerry hurried down to the deli to buy more whisky for Morag. Inside she met Dinnie.

"Hello, Kerry," said Dinnie, summoning up his courage. "I had a really nice flower for you except that stupid fairy Heather lost it somewhere."

"How dare you meddle with my flower alphabet!" shouted Kerry, and gave him a good solid punch to the face.

TWENTY

Kerry and Morag harvested a fine crop of daisies from a scrubby patch of grass on Houston Street.

They had gathered enough both for the collection and to wear in their hair. Morag also left some on the corpse of the tramp who lay dead on Fourth Street.

"How many's that now? Nine?"

Inside, Kerry studied her flower book.

"*Bellis perennis*," she said. "One of the easiest parts of my flower alphabet."

"Mmmm," said Morag, studying herself in the mirror. "I am almost convinced that daisies are the ideal adornment."

"Possibly," agreed Kerry. "But it's always hard to tell right away. When I first put a ring of tulips around my forehead I thought I would never be unhappy again, but I soon got tired of them. Tulips are not profound."

Suddenly angry she picked up her guitar and plugged it into her tiny practice amp.

"How am I going to replace my lost poppy? There's only two weeks left!"

She ran awkwardly through "Babylon." Morag stared glumly at her shattered violin and wished she could help.

Johnny Thunders, in celestial form, floated around Queens, where he was born, before visiting some old East Village haunts, musing on the subject of his lost guitar. He had a definite feeling that if he could not locate it he would never be entirely satisfied, even in Heaven. Furthermore, if he ever faced any awkward questions from one of the numerous saints in Heaven about aspects of his behavior while on Earth, he hoped to be able to play himself out of trouble. He always had before.

As he trailed down to East Fourth Street a semi-familiar tune caught his ear.

"Dear, dear," thought Johnny. "It's nice to know people still play my stuff, but that is a terrible attempt at 'Babylon.'"

Dinnie peered out his window. The four young Puerto Ricans were still kicking a ball around on the corner. Naturally, Dinnie did not approve. He regarded all sports as stupid and soccer was an especially stupid one. It was not even American.

At school, sports had been a nightmare for the unfit Dinnie. His father used to encourage him to play basketball. Dinnie would have been happy to see basketball made illegal, along with his father.

He kicked around his room. Heather was meant to be giving him a music lesson, but the famous MacPherson fiddle lay silent on the bed. She had not reappeared from her midmorning visit to the bar. No doubt she was lying drunk in some gutter.

From downstairs, the same lines of Shakespeare had been echoing up through his floor all morning. Today there was another audition and performers were trooping in and out, repeating the same unintelligible things over and over. Dinnie's hatred for community theater was reaching new heights.

Feeling at a loose end, he wondered if he should clean the cooker. He restrained the urge and diverted his attention to the television instead.

"This beautiful fourteen-carat gold chain can be yours for only sixty-three dollars!"

The jewelry in question rotated on a small turntable.

Dinnie found the sales channel particularly upsetting. He hated it when people phoned in to say how happy their new gold chain had made them.

"And you sell them so cheap! You've made my whole year feel just great!"

Dinnie changed channels.

"Any of you boys out there dream about being dressed up like a dirty little slut? Call 970 D-O-I-T, where all your fantasies come true."

The man in the ad was dressed in a white corset. It was a nice corset. It suited him. Dinnie did not approve.

The heat pounded into his room from outside. Today it was almost too hot and humid to bear. He wished he could afford air-conditioning. He wished he could afford anything. He also wished that Kerry had not punched him in the face. Dinnie might have been inexperienced but he knew that this was a poor start to a relationship. It had not made him like her any less.

Morag fluttered through the window, a pleasant sight with her eighteen-inch figure covered in bright hippie garments and her multicolored hair layered with daisies.

"Kerry, I have a potentially great bit of news."

"Yes?"

"Yes. The ghost of Johnny Thunders, the New York Dolls guitar virtuoso, was outside your window when you were playing 'Babylon.' He sympathizes with your difficulties in hitting all the notes and is scandalized that an ex-boyfriend of yours promised to teach you and then ratted on his promise. So

Johnny has offered to help you play it properly.

"In addition, he is going to give a thought to where I might get my fiddle repaired. He naturally knows about these things, having himself one time been poor, with only broken instruments to play.

"This Johnny Thunders is a splendid person, or ghost. He told me some funny stories about a place called Queens where he was born and showed me his tattoos. Even said he would keep a lookout for your poppy. In return, I will help him look for his 1958 Gibson Tiger Top, which apparently was a wonderful guitar. It is called a Tiger Top because it has stripes."

Kerry burst out laughing.

"It's true," protested the fairy. "You can't see him because he's a spirit, but I can. He is very handsome. I can see why he was such a hit with women."

Kerry laughed some more. She still did not believe Morag, but it was a good story.

She threaded a few more daisies in her hair, checking the arrangement against her poster of *Primavera*. She was pleased with the way the yellow and white of the daisies stood out against her blue hair. To please Morag and advance her plan, she was going to visit Dinnie and apologize for hitting him.

Dinnie pulled at the back of his hair. Heather was making him grow a ponytail.

"A ponytail? Are you completely out of your mind? Why the hell would I want to grow a ponytail?"

"Because Kerry likes boys with radical hairstyles," explained the fairy. "The last man she liked was Cal. Cal has a ponytail. I am sure you can grow an excellent one. I will dye it green for you."

Dinnie almost choked. The thought of him, Dinnie MacKintosh, parading around the streets with a green ponytail was so bizarre he could barely comprehend it.

"You stupid fairy. Just because she liked some jerk with a ponytail doesn't mean she's going to fall for anyone else who has one, does it?"

"Well, no, I suppose not. But it will help. I tell you, an unusual hairstyle is a must. That's the sort of boy she likes. And me and Morag, for that matter."

Dinnie, seeing that she was quite serious, became desperate. "It will take years to grow."

"No it won't." Heather was smug. "Because it just so happens that growing hair is one of the magics available to a thistle fairy. You can have a braw ponytail in no time."

She flew up behind him and touched the back of his head.

Dinnie waved his hands angrily in the air.

"Are your forgetting that this woman punched me in the eye only yesterday?"

"A mere lovers' tiff," said Heather, and departed for her midmorning dram.

On Bodmin Moor, Aelric and his band carried out a daring raid, setting fire to Tala's main cloth factory, the one that manufactured clothing for export to European fairies.

"This'll upset his balance of trade," mused Aelric, hurling his torch into the building.

But when Aelis tried to drop her propaganda leaflets she was chased off by the strong fliers posted as guards. Aelis, who was Magris's daughter, and very clever with her hands, had made the printing press, the first one ever in the hands of British fairies. The propaganda leaflets had seemed like a master stroke and it was enormously frustrating that they could not be distributed.

They were then nearly trapped by the mercenary band sent out to hunt them down. They made their getaway only by the

hand of Aelis, who magicked up a thunderstorm to cover their
retreat.

Afterwards there was some criticism of Aelric, and it was
murmured among the band that he had not planned the raid
carefully enough due to being distracted by his love for
Marion. It was even whispered that he was wasting his time
hunting for rare flowers to send her as gifts.

Dinnie picked up his fiddle. He could now play seven Scottish
tunes fairly well. He would go and busk. He'd show Heather
that she was not the only one around here who could get hold
of money.

At the bottom of the stairs he was assailed by actors' voices.

`   "Stay, gentle Helena; hear my excuse:

My love, my life, my soul, fair Helena!"

Before Dinnie could shout any abuse, Cal appeared wearing a gold crown and holding a copy of A Midsummer Night's
Dream. Dinnie ignored his greeting.

"Busking again?" said Cal, spying his violin.

Dinnie knew that Cal was laughing at him.

"I'll show him," thought Dinnie, and unslung the fiddle.

"Yes," replied Dinnie. "I have been perfecting my technique
with the help of a famous teacher. Listen to this."

`   He burst into what was meant to be a fierce rendition of
"The Miller of Drone." Unfortunately under Cal's gaze his fingers would not seem to work properly. They felt like sausages,
too big and clumsy to hold down a string. He ground to a
painful halt on the fourth bar.

"You must introduce me to your teacher," said Cal.

"Music, ho, music, such as charmeth sleep," came an
actress's voice from the next room.

"Shut the fuck up!" screamed Dinnie, assuming he was
being made fun of, although it was in fact a line from the play.

Humiliated by his performance in front of Cal he stormed blindly out of the building.

Immediately outside the door he crashed into another pedestrian and they both tumbled down the steps into the street.

Dinnie, enraged beyond endurance, picked up his fiddle and prepared to physically abuse whoever it was.

"Why can't you watch where you're going, you ignorant bitch," he screamed.

He paused. He recognized that jeweled waistcoat.

A bruised and distressed Kerry struggled to her feet, having come off much worse in the collision.

Dinnie felt faint. He had just bowled his heartthrob into the gutter.

"I guess he was still mad about the punch in the face," Kerry told Morag, checking to see that her colostomy bag had not suffered any damage.

She felt unwell after this collision and slept for the rest of the day.

Morag studied her sleeping form carefully. In her opinion Kerry's disease was getting worse. Morag had no great healing skills, apart from the normal run-of-the-mill ones possessed by all fairies, but she was sure that Kerry's health aura was starting to dim, and wondered if another major attack was on the way.

TWENTY-ONE

It was midnight in Central Park and the fairies were lying around smoking their pipes and drinking whisky. Brannoc sat with Petal, teaching her "The Liverpool Hornpipe," which he had learned long ago from a traveling Northern piper fairy. Petal struggled to get her fingers around the notes. So did Tulip, though Brannoc was not teaching him.

"That is not a bad tune at all," said Maeve from behind her tree, and ran through it gently on her whistle. She had entirely forgotten her argument with Brannoc, though he had not.

Padraig took up the tune on his whistle. Both he and Maeve had quick ears and could play anything after the briefest of hearings. Petal and Tulip were slower, but it did not take them too long to learn, and soon the jaunty sound of "The Liverpool Hornpipe" was filling their grove. When they had played it through a few times Maeve started in with another hornpipe they all knew, "The Boys of Bluehill," and the nocturnal animals danced their way around the clearing as they went about their business.

"Now, what is that," said Spiro, looking upwards. A curve of grey in seven shades was descending from the sky to the ground.

"You ever see anything like that?"

'Of course," said Brannoc. "It's a moonbow. From the rain at night."

"Well, what's it doing here? It hasn't been raining."

Brannoc shrugged.

"Oh, no," said sharp-eyed Tulip. "They're coming down the moonbow."

Out of the sky came twenty-one Cornish mercenaries, marching in good order.

The black fairies lived, unseen by any humans apart from a few wise old women, in a small park on 114th street. The park was in disrepair, uncared for by the city authorities, but it was well known for its air of peace and very rarely did anything unpleasant happen there.

They were holding a council meeting after learning that there had been a further incursion into their territory, presumably hostile.

"They both had swords. We pursued them but they escaped on a bike."

The piece of news prompted a stormy discussion. Some were in favor of marching down through the city and teaching the Italian fairies a lesson. Others felt they should let the matter pass in the interests of peace.

Their sage took note of their counsel and considered the matter. Her name was Okailey, and she was a direct descendant of the fairies who flourished in the powerful African empire of Ghana, as long ago as the fourth century.

A troop of young girls wound their way through the park, all in blue uniforms on an outing from school. They caught the fairies' aura and laughed as they passed.

"These happy school children would have more sense than to march off and wage war," said their sage. "And so should we. But I don't think we should ignore the matter entirely. I will lead a delegation down south to visit the Italians—"

"They might have been agents of the Chinese."

"—Or Chinese. And we will sort things out in a reasonable manner."

This decided, they made ready to leave. For the community of Ghanaian fairies this was a major event. They had never in living memory been south of Central Park.

"Who are they," hissed Padraig, shrinking back into the arms of his lover Maeve.

"English mercenaries," whimpered Tulip, who recognized several of the band from Cornwall. "Paid by Tala the King."

The five stared in alarm as the mercenaries strode down the moonbow. So accurate was Magris's conjuring that they were coming to ground less than a hundred yards away and had already spotted the fugitives.

"Right," said Maeve, standing up and drawing her sword. "I'll teach them to come chasing me over water."

"Are you mad?" protested Tulip. "They'll cut us to pieces. We'll have to flee."

"An O'Brien fairy does not flee from anything," said the Irish fairy. "Particularly Maeve O'Brien, finest sword in Galway."

Petal burst into tears. She was far from the finest sword in Cornwall and she did not want to be cut into pieces.

Brannoc was of a mind to fight himself, being generally so depressed about his futile passion for Petal that going down in a last desperate battle did not seem to be a bad thing. The sight of Petal in tears changed his mind.

"We are too outnumbered," he said. "We'll have to run."

Padraig agreed, to the extreme displeasure of Maeve.

"No O'Brien fairy has ever fled from danger before. Padraig, I am ashamed of you."

This brief disagreement almost cost the fairies their chance to flee. The Co Sidth dogs were loosed from their chains and bounded toward them. Maeve stepped forward and killed two of them with two thrusts of her sword. The third fled in confusion.

How about that, thought Brannoc. She really can use her sword.

They fled through the undergrowth, running, hopping, climbing and fluttering their way south as far down the park as they could go before stumbling to an exhausted halt near the exit at East Fifty-ninth. There they collapsed on the ground, unable to go any farther.

Some way behind the mercenaries on the moonbow had been the MacLeod sisters. When the warriors in front of them had marched down to the ground, the MacLeods had leapt from the moonbow high in the air and floated to the ground, unseen by anyone.

They had been aware of the events below them, and had seen Maeve killing the dogs, but hurried on to the far edge of the park, for there they had seen something far more interesting to them – Heather and Morag, their prey, busy escaping from an angry mob of black fairies by riding on the back of a bike.

The MacLeods had almost caught them by following suit. Had it not been for the intervention of their strange ally with the shopping bag, they would have succeeded. They sat now in Union Square, acclimatizing themselves to this bizarre new city and preparing to continue the hunt.

Back in Central Park the mercenaries, prepared only to face a few fugitives, were surprised to find themselves completely surrounded by a large tribe of black fairies.

Too outnumbered to fight, they were taken prisoner by their equally puzzled adversaries, who could not quite understand who these interlopers were.

TWENTY-TWO

The day quickly grew hot and damp. Morag, awake as usual hours before Kerry, mopped her brow and wondered if she could reasonably remove several thousand dollars from a bank to buy Kerry air conditioning.

Feeling just too hot to lie around she went out to see what she could find. She found Heather in the corner deli, eyeing up a bottle of whisky, unsure how to open it.

"Your drinking is getting out of control," said Morag.

"A MacKintosh's drinking is never out of control," replied Heather, stiffly. "Not that it is any of your damn business. No doubt you are here for the same reason."

"I am not. I am here to get some bagels."

"What are bagels?"

"Bready things. I rip bits off them for breakfast sometimes and then the people in the delis think they're damaged and they give them to tramps outside. Have you noticed how many people here just live on the streets?"

"Of course. I spend half my time finding food and change for them. Have you noticed how they keep dying on Fourth Street?"

Morag had. Around ten since she arrived.

"What will we do about the MacLeods?"

It was frightening to be in the same city as the sisters. They were bound to be caught.

It was a time for shared thought and concerted action. So, naturally, they began to argue about whose fault it all was. Morag ripped some pieces from the bagels and departed haughtily.

Heather was unsure what do with herself. It was not safe to linger in the street with so many enemies everywhere, but it was equally unsafe in Dinnie's rooms. He had been upset to the point of violence ever since Heather had walked in unannounced while he was masturbating in front of the television.

"Get out of here, you disgusting little spy!" he screamed.

"I was not spying. I was exhibiting the natural curiosity of a thistle fairy in alien surroundings."

Dinnie was not placated by this and carried out a savage attack with his bicycle pump. Heather fluttered to the other side of the room.

"You are risking tragedy, you know. A roused fairy is a dangerous thing."

"I'll rouse this bicycle pump right up your ass."

"You are breaking the bargain."

"I'll break your neck."

Heather regretted purloining enough dollars for Dinnie to buy a new bike. She decided that she'd better not go back for a while and departed to the bar to watch baseball. Inside she was pleased to discover that the Yankees were two up at the top of the seventh and next up was their best left-handed hitter.

Morag and Kerry had been visiting friends of Kerry's, all of whom were unwell. Kerry talked brightly to them while the unseen Morag used her fairy powers to help them.

They called on a friend who had a terrible toothache and Morag touched his jaw and cured it, which was just as well as he had no money to go to a dentist. They visited a friend who had hurt his back moving an amplifier and could not get out of bed. Morag gently massaged his spine, producing a miracle cure, which was good as he had no money to go to a doctor.

They called on a young woman who was perpetually nervous and agoraphobic after being attacked on the street and Morag gently sang a soothing Highland air into her subconscious, thereby bringing her great comfort, which was a relief as she had no money to go to a therapist.

After this Kerry was abnormally tired and went home to bed while Morag hung around on the rooftops.

On the fire escape, Morag had a sudden insight that something was wrong. She rushed upstairs to find Kerry being sick on the bedclothes. She was vomiting continually and had already developed a high fever. Morag knew that this was beyond her powers of healing and called an ambulance.

Kerry was taken away to the hospital where they diagnosed an abscess in her intestines brought on by the Crohn's disease. This had poisoned her system and would kill her if not treated immediately. Surgeons re-opened the twelve-inch scar on her stomach and removed another small piece of her digestive system.

Sitting next to her at the hospital, Morag was sad. She hated to see Kerry as pale as death with a drip in her arm and a tube running up her nose, a catheter attached to her urethra and another tube coming out of her stomach, draining away the poison.

She reflected that it was fortunate Kerry had such comprehensive health insurance; what happened to people without health insurance if they got Crohn's disease, Morag could not imagine.

TWENTY-THREE

Friendly birds told the Chinese fairies of widespread troubles; strange fairies were marching and fighting in New York.

Lu-Tang, their sage, a dignified fairy whose white and yellow wings folded neatly over her blue silk tunic, was worried. Neither she nor any of her community knew what to make of it all.

"But it is all the more reason for us to recover the mirror."

With troubles around it was most unfortunate for the Bhat Gwa to be lost. It was time for the Festival of Hungry Ghosts when malevolent spirits were liable to appear. The Chinese fairies did not want to be facing malevolent spirits without the protection of their Bhat Gwa mirror.

The mirror was at present hidden safely in Magenta's bag and Magenta was marching through the foothills of Fourth Avenue, keeping an eye out for Joshua and his Persian hordes, and also the Armenians, fierce local tribesmen.

There were a great deal of fierce local tribesmen on the streets of New York and Magenta was continually harassed. The worst ones had blue shirts and guns and they never seemed to leave her alone.

Joshua was some streets behind, still searching for her. He asked every tramp he met if they had seen her. Some of them gave him drinks from their bottles, sympathetic to his poor state of health now he no longer had his Fitzroy cocktail to rely on.

The Cornish mercenaries were meanwhile marching back over the Atlantic to England, having failed in their mission. The Ghanaian tribe were too peaceable to be interested in taking prisoners and were happy to just send them back. They assumed that they had now rid their city of hostile elements and were pleased that they were not facing trouble from their fellow New York fairies.

Unfortunately, the Cu Sidth dog which escaped Maeve's blade was not captured but bolted through Central Park and followed the scent of the fleeing Scots fairies. Somewhere around Sixteenth Street it came upon two young Italian fairies who had separated from the scouting party to romance in peace on a fire escape. Crazed in the city the dog mauled them before help arrived and the beast ran off.

The Italians were furious. They assumed that their shadowy enemies had sent the dog to attack them. Scenting that it came from the north, they gathered their tribe and prepared to march.

Morag tried to make Kerry as comfortable as possible by feeding her soup and chattering away brightly. She told her tales of Scotland's history and great fairies of the past. She told her what was happening on the street outside, and what was in the newspapers – but as what was in the newspapers was generally more trouble in the Middle East or Texas abortion clinics being bombed by fanatics, this was not a great success.

"On the positive side," continued Morag, reading the paper, "Delta airlines are offering special cheap tickets if you want to fly round America with a friend."

Morag put the paper down.

"Let's talk about sex," she said. "I know you like talking about sex."

"You're right," said Kerry. "You start."

Morag said she saw a strange thing while visiting Dinnie's room.

"An advert came on his television where a naked woman was being pissed over. You had to phone up a special number—970 P-I-S-S, I think—to hear more about it."

Kerry said she hoped the young fairy was not shocked by seeing such a thing.

"It was all right," said Morag, not wanting Kerry to think she was backward in any way. "Urine fetishism is not unknown among fairies. I believe that among MacKintoshes it is quite popular.

"But I did see a book in a shop, the exact meaning of which eludes me. It was called *Lesbian Foot Fetishists—The Movie*. What, exactly, does this entail?"

Kerry explained, making Morag laugh. She said that men in Scotland would not be so stupid as to read such things, and Kerry answered she had no doubt they would be if given the chance.

"Where did you see such a book?"

"I went into a sex shop for a look around. I didn't like the sex books at all but I was interested to learn that humans did oral sex."

She had imagined they would be too clumsy and might hurt each other with their big teeth.

"I suppose fairies are good at it?"

"Of course. I am a noted expert."

"What a little goldmine of talent you are, Morag."

Kerry struggled out of bed.

"Nine days left," she said. "I must have my poppy back. Where is it?"

"With Magenta, who is walking the streets hiding from the Persian army. You are not well enough to look for her."

"I will tear them apart for this," growled Ailsa, eldest of the MacLeod sisters. She glared balefully around her at the hateful city landscape. They were now stranded on a tree in Washington Square Park, and they did not like it at all.

"This place is a nightmare," said Seónaid.

"How will we get home?"

"Where are the MacKintosh and the MacPherson?"

Ailsa shook her head. She did not know. Having lived most of their life on the Isle of Skye they were even less used to cities than Heather and Morag. The confusion of the place interfered with Mairi's second sight and she could not yet locate their prey. When crossing the moonbow they had not been prepared for such a place. Now they were tired and hungry. Their MacLeod kilts were mud-stained and torn from the chase though the park and streets.

Ailsa, like her sisters a most beautiful fairy with a proud face under her jagged hair, unsheathed her claymore and slid from the tree to the ground.

"We need food and drink. Follow me."

Seónaid, Mairi and Rhona followed. They were wary, though not afraid. Mairi sniffed the air.

"That woman who helped Heather and Morag is close. I can sense it." She sniffed the air again. "And that man over the road is following her."

The MacLeods fluttered across the road and floated gently behind Joshua.

Aelric picked some tulips, some daffodils and a bunch of wild thyme.

"Very pretty," said Aelis, knowing they were for the King's

stepdaughter. "I'm sure she'll love them. However, aren't you meant to be hard at work in the library, learning how to carry out the next phase of the peasants' revolution?"

"It was half-day closing."

"Fine," said Aelis. "But I imagine Chairman Mao still did something useful even on half-day closing. Come and help me print leaflets."

Today, Aelric's heart wasn't in the revolution, even though his band of followers had grown to twenty. He spent all his time thinking about Marion, and passing secret messages to her via their contact at court.

TWENTY-FOUR

Dinnie's ponytail grew extraordinarily quickly, to his great distress. When Heather struggled in one day with a tube of blue hair dye he locked himself in the bathroom.

"Go away," he shouted through the door. "I have already suffered enough today."

"How?"

"I memorized all the tracks on the first two Slayer albums."

"I quite liked them," replied Heather, and proceeded to bully and blackmail Dinnie into letting her in.

"There," she said afterwards. "What a braw color."

Dinnie was horrified.

"It's awful. You never said anything about blue ponytails when we made this agreement."

"I said I would take all steps necessary. It's not my fault you chose to fall in love with a fan of bright clothes, psychedelia and hair dye. If you'd fallen for a young executive I'd have dressed you up in a suit. As it is, let's go and try you out on the world."

They trooped downstairs. If Cal appeared and laughed at him, Dinnie swore he would beat him over the head, probably with Heather.

They walked to the health food store. Heather ignored Dinnie's customary complaints about the horrors of alfalfa and veggie burgers and concentrated on studying the reactions of suitable young women as Dinnie passed. Did those two young punks on the corner show just a flicker of interest as he strode by? Possibly.

Although still overweight, he had lost most of his double chin. His posture was better and, clean-shaven, he looked years younger. She had forbidden him to wear his old brown trousers and though she had still not come up with a suitable replacement for his voluminous brown coat, he was undoubtedly looking more attractive. Heather was pleased. At least this part of her plan was working.

"Do you have a nickel, sir?" a tramp pleaded as they passed.

"Fuck you," muttered Dinnie.

Heather coughed.

Dinnie dropped some change into his cup.

"Doesn't that make you feel good?" asked Heather, to which Dinnie grunted an unintelligible reply.

Cornwall was wet and very cold, but in the workhouses the fairies were well wrapped up. Although they no longer had freedom, the new spinning machines had greatly increased production and there was more cloth for cloaks and blankets.

Tala the King was in council with Magris and his barons, discussing trade. The French fairies across the Channel in Breton were keen to import Tala's cloth and had placed a large order. Unfortunately this order could no longer be met due to Aelric destroying the cloth factory. The discussion was interrupted by news of the return of the mercenaries from America.

Tala was furious at the failure. He abandoned discussion of exchange rates and insisted that new plans were laid to recapture the fugitives.

This was frustrating for Magris, who had been anxious to

put before the king his plan for a large fairy township which he saw as the next logical step in their society's development.

Tala would not listen to this now and demanded that Magris immediately devise a strategy for a general invasion of New York. If necessary he would send the entire English fairy host across the Atlantic.

"Look at this propaganda leaflet!" he thundered. "It proclaims Petal and Tulip as he rightful rulers of the Cornish fairy kingdom! What will happen if these leaflets are successfully distributed? While that pair are still alive, the rebel Aelric will always be able to make trouble."

The assistant at the health food store fumbled with Dinnie's change. Dinnie opened his mouth to complain but noticing Heather's warning look he smiled instead, and waited patiently.

"Did you recognize him?" the assistant asked her fellow worker as Dinnie left. "He seemed to remind me of someone, but I can't think who."

"Nice looking guy anyway. Great ponytail."

As they walked back down First Avenue Heather announced that perhaps it was no bad thing that Dinnie had knocked Kerry down the stairs. After all, it now gave him an excellent reason to strike up a conversation.

"You can apologize for being such a clumsy oaf and then subtly work the conversation round to the first two Slayer albums. While you're doing it, be sure she gets a good view of your hip new hairstyle. You'll start to impress her right away."

Dinnie thought that this was all a little simplistic and began to wonder if the fairy had ever matched up a pair of lovers in her life. Possibly some village idiots in Cruickshank.

As they turned onto Fourth Street they saw Kerry and Morag coming out of the deli.

"Now is your chance," whispered Heather.

They met on the sidewalk.

"Hello, Kerry," said Dinnie. "I'm real sorry I bounced you down the stairs. It was an accident."

"That's all right. I'm sorry I punched you in the face."

There was a short silence.

"I've just been listening to the first two Slayer albums. Fine stuff."

Kerry smiled encouragingly. Unfortunately Dinnie's conversation then ground to a halt. He could not think of what to say next. Kerry's smiling had put him off completely, because it was a lovely smile.

They faced each other in awkward silence.

"Well, good," said Kerry finally. "I like them as well."

"Right," said Dinnie. "Excellent records."

"Yes," agreed Kerry.

"I must be off," said Dinnie, and departed quickly.

"Why did you run away," protested Heather, back indoors.

"I felt stupid. I didn't know what to say. I was drowning in my own sweat."

Heather told Dinnie off from force of habit, but she did not really mind that he had not made much of the conversation. She knew that prospective lovers often found each other's company a little awkward at first. Quite possibly Kerry would prefer a man who was a little shy to one who was too full of himself. The important thing was that he had made a start.

She reassured Dinnie that this had been a reasonable beginning.

"My plan is working fine. I got the distinct feeling she likes you."

Heather looked forward to fulfilling her part of the bargain and gaining the fiddle.

Across the street Kerry was slightly shaky after her first trip outside since her illness. She drank tea with Morag.

"I'm sorry I couldn't do better with Dinnie," she said. "But I was feeling a little weak. Also he seemed difficult to talk to."

"That's all right, Kerry. I thought you did fine. If I'm going to convince Dinnie that you've fallen in love with him it wouldn't do for you to be too enthusiastic at first. He might be suspicious. He will know from experience that women do not fall in love with him right away. Just keep smiling at him and we'll fool him easily. I am already looking forward to fulfilling my part of the bargain and gaining the fiddle."

The MacLeod sisters sat in Joshua's shopping cart as he pursued Magenta along West Twenty-third and down Sixth Avenue.

"Hurry," hissed Ailsa. "You're catching up."

Joshua stepped up his pace. He did not really understand why four Scottish fairies had come to his aid in his pursuit of Magenta, but as they were liberal with their whisky and cunning in obtaining food, they were welcome to trail along.

TWENTY-FIVE

Morag was also out hunting for Magenta, but in the large city she could not find her.

She sat, dispirited, watching some squirrels in Madison Square.

"Hello, fairy."

It was Johnny Thunders.

Morag repressed an urge to giggle. She found Johnny Thunders unusually attractive and regretted that he was four times as tall as her, and a ghost.

"You look sad."

Morag explained all the latest developments. Johnny sympathized.

"I'm having a hard time myself. I can't see any sign of my guitar. If I even passed the building it was in, I'd know, but it's gone. Still, I think I can help you. I remember down in Chinatown there was an instrument maker could fix anything. Hwui-Yin. To look at him you wouldn't think he knew what an electric guitar was, but one time he fixed one of my favorites when it was just about totally destroyed after a Dolls gig at the Mercer Arts Center."

Morag shook her head. She remembered the name.

"I can't go there without being lynched by Chinese fairies."

"Nonsense. Hwui-Yin was a good friend of mine. I'll see you're all right. Hop on my shoulder and we'll float on down."

With the aid of the MacLeods, Joshua was able to cunningly corner Magenta at west Fourteenth.

"Okay, Magenta. Hand it over."

"Never, Tissaphernes."

"Stop being crazy and hand it over."

The MacLeods meanwhile dived into Magenta's shopping bag, hoping that it still contained Heather and Morag, but emerged looking frustrated.

"Where are they?"

"An Athenian nobleman does not rat on his associates," replied Magenta, stiffly.

"Oh yeah?" sneered Joshua. "Xenophon would have. For an Athenian he was very fond of the Spartans."

"This is entirely beside the point. He was brought up fully in line with the high standard of conduct expected of an Athenian."

Bored with this, the MacLeod sisters began to drift off.

"Hey," said Joshua. "Where are you going?"

Xenophon, a general renowned for his military cunning, saw his chance. While Tissaphernes talked with his allies, she sprinted for a cab, wrenched open the door and disappeared at speed.

"So where are Heather and Morag?" muttered Seónaid as they floated up to the sixth floor of a handy fire escape.

None of them knew. They would have to start their hunt anew.

"What is that, Rhona?"

"A flower," replied the youngest sister, who was not always so serious as the others. "I found it in the old lady's shopping bag. I feel that it is a powerful thing."

She looked happily at the triple-bloom, the most pleasant thing she had seen since arriving in New York.

Heather was in a bad mood. She had just seen Morag returning from what seemed to have been a wild drunken celebration with a group of Chinese fairies.

"I can't understand it," she complained to Dinnie. "Back in Scotland she was the quiet one. Now, not content with being the girl about town with Kerry, she is out partying with the Chinese. How did she manage that? Last week they were trying to kill us. How come she is having fun all the time while I am stuck here with you?"

"I expect it's her pleasant manner," said Dinnie. "No doubt she treats her friends well instead of forcing them to eat vegetables and listen to endless tapes of Sonic Youth."

Heather was not at all pleased. She had not liked the way some of these Chinese fairies were looking at Morag.

"Hello, Kerry," shrieked Morag, and fell on the floor drunk. "Guess what. My fiddle is being fixed by a clever man in Chinatown. He is a friend of Johnny Thunders. He is also a friend of the fairies and I explained everything away and now they like me. I have four dates for next week.

"Furthermore, I have brought you a bloom from the *Polygonum multiflorum* which I cleverly remembered appears in your alphabet. It grows in China, but the Chinese fairies had lots of them. And not only that,"—she raised herself on her elbow—"Johnny Thunders played me the guitar solo from 'Bad Girl.' Slowly. I now have it in my head and will teach you it when I'm sober. He is a wonderful guitarist. Have you seen a 1958 Gibson Tiger Top guitar anywhere? No?"

Morag folded her wings untidily behind her and dropped into unconsciousness.

"I am sick of being stuck here alone," declared Heather. "I am going to make some fairy friends of my own."

"Oh yeah? Who?"

"The Italians."

Dinnie laughed.

"You told me they were after you for robbing their banks."

"I shall rectify the situation."

Heather sat down in front of the mirror, spat on it to clean away the dust, and took a tiny ivory comb out of her sporran. She got to work on her hair, combing it out till it hung down golden and crimson almost to her waist.

"What are you going to do? Grovel and apologize?"

"No," replied Heather. "A MacKintosh fairy does not need to grovel and apologize to put right a little misunderstanding. I shall find out who is important in the Italian tribe, then I'll flirt with them."

"Flirt with them?"

"That's right. Works every time."

TWENTY-SIX

In Central Park Petal and Tulip were receiving instruction in swordplay from Maeve.

"Parry. Lunge. Parry. Lunge."

The young English fairies parried and lunged.

Brannoc and Padraig shared a pipe under a tree. They new home at the south end of Central Park beside the pong was noisier than their last, but they were getting used to the humans everywhere around.

"It's no use moping about Petal all day," said Padraig. "Have you told her you're in love with her?"

Brannoc had not. Nor did he intend to.

"You can't spend the rest of your life hiding up a tree playing sad tunes on the flute, can you?"

Brannoc did not see why not. He was stuck in a foreign country pining over a fairy who spent half her time having sex with her brother. What else was there to do? He looked on at the sword practice, feeling vaguely that he could teach Petal just as well, but somehow never got the chance.

Maeve hit Tulip on the head with the flat of her blade after he made a particularly feeble attempt at parrying her attack.

"No good at all," she cried. "Hopeless. If I'd tried parrying like that the time three Firbolgs attacked me in Connacht they wouldn't have known whether to cut my head off or fall about laughing."

"Why did they attack you?" panted Tulip, trying to catch his breath.

Maeve shrugged. "Firbolgs are unpredictable creatures."

"Especially when you cheat them at dice," called Padraig.

"Yes," laughed Maeve. "Especially when you cheat them at dice. But they cheated first. And it was still a mighty battle, even if it was only over a game of dice. I fought them with swords, knives, bits of magic and bits of wood over three counties before they gave up and fled. My hands were so sore and bloodied it was three weeks before I could play music again.

"Which is how I got together with Padraig, really, as he told me afterwards that he'd been trying to catch my attention for months but could never make himself heard over the sound of my pipes."

Sword practice ended and Maeve came over to play music with Padraig. Petal and Tulip departed into the bushes. Brannoc felt left out as usual and flew off to wander on his own. Petal's white wings had looked particularly attractive while she was fencing, but this only depressed him further.

He was not, however, as depressed as the fairies across the ocean in Cornwall. They were all being drafted into the army. Tala was preparing a vast fairy host to march across the Atlantic, defeat whatever foreign fairies he found, and recapture his children.

Everywhere there was misery. Red Caps with dogs policed the invisible kingdom and any resistance was quickly put down.

Magris always made a point of saying that it was not compulsory for the fairies to work in his workhouses. This was true, but as it was forbidden to leave Cornwall, and as all the fairies' land was now in the hands of the landowners, there was no way of growing or gathering food, and the choice was between working for wages or starving.

Now, as the army mustered, the looms ceased and production came to a halt.

Brannoc, fluttering north through the park, would have been aware that things were bad in England had he thought about it, but he was too involved in thinking about Petal to notice much else. He had a fierce desire to wrap his wings around her and carry her off to a lonely tree-top somewhere. However, he would never do this. He was too polite. Also, Petal would strongly object.

He settled down disconsolately on a tree and there, on the ground below him, were four black fairies asleep on the grass. Brannoc's first impulse was to flee.

No, he thought. I won't. It is stupid for us to be enemies. I will go and talk to them.

Maeve and Padraig, as was customary with fairies, slept through the latter part of the day to awaken at dusk and play music.

They woke, kissed and poured out a little whisky to set the night in motion. Petal and Tulip emerged from behind a bush to join them.

"Where's Brannoc?"

No one knew.

A furtive bag lady trundled her shopping trolley through the bushes, looking carefully to the left and right. The fairies were interested in this. They had seen her several times, and each time she passed, an equally strange-looking man followed after her.

A fairy-like shape plummeted through the branches above, hovered for a second, then plunged to the earth with a thud.

"Brannoc! What happened?"

Brannoc raised himself weakly on his elbows.

"I met the black fairies," he mumbled.

"Did they hurt you badly?"

"No," gasped Brannoc. "We made friends. But they had some terribly potent alcohol."

He slumped back to the ground, and began to snore.

A slight breeze stirred in the park.

TWENTY-SEVEN

Dinnie pulled on his ragged leather jacket in his clumsy manner and looked in the mirror with disgust. This jacket, the source of yet another bitter argument between him and Heather, had been picked out especially for him by the fairy at a second-hand clothes shop just opposite the Canal Street post office.

While there, Heather had been interested to see that on the walls of the post office were posters from the FBI giving details of wanted criminals.

"Well, I never," she mused, studying the hardened faces staring out at her. "This country is in serious condition. What you need is PC MacBain from Cruickshank. He would soon sort them out. He'd give them a guid scone on the lug."

"A brilliant solution," said Dinnie, sarcastically.

Dinnie did not want a leather jacket, but Heather briskly bullied him into it. The fairy's patience was today even thinner than usual as she was still rather hungover from the party with her new Italian friends. She had been sick all morning, although she insisted to Dinnie that this was only because she was not used to pasta. They argued briefly, bought the jacket and returned home.

Tonight Dinnie had his first date with Kerry. It had not been difficult to arrange, although Dinnie went through a nightmare of nerves verging on complete panic when Heather maneuvered him into it. She had led him to the deli when Kerry was there, then whispered in his ear that either he asked her out this very minute or she was leaving immediately with the fiddle.

"And I can fly to your room quicker than you can climb the stairs."

To Dinnie's surprise, even after he had stuttered what must have been one of the most graceless and uninviting requests for a date in human history, Kerry happily agreed.

They were to meet that night at ten and go to hear some music in a club. Dinnie was extremely pleased, and very anxious.

Across the road, Morag was also pleased.

"Thank you, Kerry," she said. "I regard this as a great favor. Are you sure you don't mind going out with him too much?"

Kerry shook her head.

"It's okay, Morag. There'll be lots of my friends at the club anyway, so I won't be bored."

"It won't make you very unhappy turning up at some hip place with that big lump trailing after you? I wouldn't want to ruin your credibility."

"No, it's fine," promised Kerry. "Anyway, he doesn't look too bad these days. He seems to have a lost a lot of weight."

"And grown a nice pony tail."

While Kerry was out with Dinnie, Morag was going to pick up with her fiddle from Hwui-Yin. Then she intended to show the Chinese fairies what a Scottish fiddler could do.

Tala the King's palace was made of trees grown together to form rooms and courtyards. Formerly a pleasant and open place, it was now dark and heavily guarded.

Aelric crept silently past the guards. He was coated in a substance which made his aura dim to other fairies and his scent undetectable to guard dogs.

He climbed swiftly up a solid oak to where he knew the bedroom of Marion was and peered through the leaf-covered window space.

Marion had long black hair covered in light-blue beads. This stretched like a cape down to her thighs. She was busy in her bedroom singing a preserving song to a cut flower. Aelric muttered a brief prayer to the Goddess and hopped inside.

Heather spent the first part of the evening feeling elated because her plan was working so well and she would soon have the MacPherson fiddle in her hands, and the second part in dejection because she realized that Dinnie would probably ruin everything.

It was all very well getting him a date with Kerry, but after that it was up to him, and he was not a man to inspire confidence. She shuddered to think of the awful things Dinnie might do on a date with Kerry. He might get drunk and when he got drunk he tended to dribble beer down his chin. This was not a pleasant sight. He might suddenly lose control of his appetite and be overwhelmed by the urge to immediately buy and eat a family-sized bag of peanut and pistachio cookies. He had done this before, and it was not a pleasant sight, either.

He could do worse things. He might insult Kerry's friends. He might swear at a beggar in the street. He might shout abuse at the band, even though Kerry liked them. He might be too mean to share a cab home. Kerry would not like any of those things.

Worst of all, he might try to grope her, something Heather had expressly forbidden as he went out of the door but still worried about terribly.

"If you grope this young woman on your first date, it's the end of everything," she said to his departing figure. "Do not grope her. She'll hate it. Have a nice time."

Oh well. There was nothing she could do about it now

except wait. She flew down to the bar to drink and watch base-ball.

Warmed by a few drams, things did not seem so bad. She knew that Dinnie would not be perfect, but his failings were essential to her plan. She was aware that a perfect Dinnie would be a bore, and this would be almost as bad as an appallingly badly behaved Dinnie. Heather was counting on the recent behavioral changes she had worked in Dinnie making enough of a difference to make him attractive, without the rough edges entirely disappearing.

"Which is a damn subtle plan, when you come to think of it," she said to herself, meanwhile applauding a fine Yankees grounder that advanced the man on first right round to the third. "And well worthy of success."

"Yes," agreed the numerous Chinese fairies who surrounded Morag, plying her with drinks. "Your friend's plan to win the East Fourth Street Community Arts Prize sounds worthy of success. Of course we will try and help. Just bring us a list of the flowers you still need and we'll find them for you. And we will keep a look out for this Magenta woman who thinks she is Xenophon and see if we can retrieve the poppy."

Attracted by this brilliantly colored visitor from across the ocean, they were eager to please.

"You are very kind," said Morag, pouring down a few more Chinese beers. "Possibly while you're at it you could keep an eye open for a 1958 Gibson Tiger Top with 'Johnny Thunders' stenciled on the back."

"We already are," said the Chinese. "When Johnny Thunders' ghost brought you here he asked us to help, and we will. We had been fans of his ever since he recorded 'Chinese Rocks,' although we know the Dee Dee Ramone claims to have written it."

Aelric joined his rebel band, now numbering thirty, just in time for the night's raid. Half of them were to stage a phony attack on a grain barn to distract the mercenary band who were hunting them, while the other half were to carry out the real attack on Magris's new weapon factory, where swords, shields and spears were now being produced at a frightening rate.

"So," asked Aelis, buckling on her breastplate, "how was the King's stepdaughter?"

"Wonderful. I told her I love her."

"What did she say?"

"She said I was a disgusting rebel who was ruining her beloved father's kingdom and I ought to have my head cut off. Then she pulled a knife and attacked me while simultaneously screaming out for the guards. She is a very resourceful young fairy."

The two groups prepared to move out.

"So is this the end of the romance?"

Aelric looked pained.

"Of course not. A passionate young fairy like myself does not let a little thing like a knife attack put him off. I shall just have to find some way of winning her heart. Her huge collection of preserved flowers for instance. I could steal them and refuse to give them back until she falls in love with me."

Aelis shook her head.

"Aelric, that it really dumb. You are a good rebel leader but a terrible romancer. What you should do is melt her heart by appearing with a spectacular addition to her collection."

Heather had told Dinnie that to all practical purposes he could presume that Kerry was in love with him when she took him in her arms and kissed him passionately, without being asked. This seemed to her a reasonable yardstick and Dinnie, for want of anything better, agreed.

She heard him clumping up the stairs. Terror welled up in her chest. He had done something dreadful and Kerry never wanted to see him again.

"Well?" she demanded.

"It was fine," said Dinnie. He was obviously pleased with himself.

"Fine?"

"Yes, fine."

They had had a pleasant evening drinking with Kerry's friends before going to hear a band at a tiny club on Avenue C. He had pretended to like the band as they were Kerry's friends, and the two of them had got on very well the whole night.

"No arguments?"

"No."

"No signs of disgust on her part?"

"No."

"Any hint of possible sexual excitement between you?"

"Yes, I think so. And we've arranged another date."

Heather clapped him heartily on the shoulder. Dinnie was equally delighted. As he took of his leather jacket he remarked that really it was a fairly good jacket as leather jackets go, and Kerry had complimented his ponytail. For the first time ever he thanked Heather, then slumped into the bed to dream happily of his next date.

"It was okay," Kerry told Morag. "No problem at all really. Dinnie was all right to be with. I don't think he liked the band much, but he was polite about it. He even made me laugh sometimes. I quite liked him."

TWENTY-EIGHT

Magenta sat down to rest at Stuyvesant Square. Not for the first time, she wished that she had more archers in her army. These winged demons who flew with the Persians were a dreadful menace.

A large family had gathered on the benches in front of her and were having heated discussions about something or other.

One thin middle-aged man, left out of the discussions, tried to encourage a young nephew to box. He continually pulled at his sleeve top to gain his attention, then threw pretend punches and put up a guard, but the nephew was not interested and turned away. The uncle would not be put off and persisted in trying to show the uninterested child how to box. Eventually the child scurried off to his mother. His mother absent-mindedly spat on a handkerchief and scrubbed his face. The uncle looked faintly disgusted and hunted around for someone else to bother.

Magenta had a vague memory of her parents trying to get her to do things she did not want to do, then hunted about in her shopping trolley. Supplies were low. She had no money to replenish her Fitzroy cocktail and during the last engagement she had lost the precious triple-bloomed flower. This was a source of immense annoyance. Back in Greece the rare flower would have fetched a great price, thereby enabling her to pay her fellow mercenaries a decent bonus. Already they were grumbling about not being paid.

Now the army had hardly anything left. All there was in her shopping trolley was the recipe for the cocktail, a supply of old newspapers, the Bhat Gwa mirror and the two pieces of the guitar she had picked up after the riot at the festival in Tompkins Square.

With one week left till judgment day, Cal's production of *A Midsummer Night's Dream* was coming along reasonably well. The four lovers wandered the imaginary woods, lost in their confused emotional affairs. Puck danced this way and that, casting around bewilderment, while Oberon and Titania, the Fairy King and Queen, quarreled mightily over the Indian boy.

Cal was particularly pleased with the new actress who was playing Titania. A young woman from Texas, currently serving meals in a diner, she was radiant and charismatic in her costume, and seemed to Cal every inch the Fairy Queen.

"She is rubbish," thought Heather crossly, watching from the wings. "More like a plate of porridge than a Fairy Queen."

Heather regarded this actress, and all the other clumsy humans playing fairy parts, as something of an insult.

The Chinese fairies, well into the swing of their festival—this is to say, drunk—received heartening news from some of the scouts.

"We have located the old woman named Magenta. Or rather, the fairly young muscular woman who looks old because she is so dirty. We tried to examine her shopping bag but in this we were not entirely successful because so much exposure to fairies has rendered her capable of seeing us.

"However, before she attacked us with rocks, we did see a glint of our precious mirror in the bag. She must have found it at the same time as she found the poppy. What is more, in her bag are two pieces of an old guitar."

Morag wiped beer from her lips.

"Could this guitar possibly be—"

"Who knows? This woman is obviously a person of great cosmic importance. The way she draws all these vital artifacts to her is clearly part of some greater plan."

Morag leapt up and drew her sword.

"Well, let's go and take them."

The Chinese were a little shocked at this. They pointed out that they were good fairies and could not just go around robbing humans when it suited them. Morag was chastened. She had forgotten this. The pressures of the big city had got to her.

"We will have to go and bargain for them."

TWENTY-NINE

Morag had a date with three Chinese and Heather had a date with four Italians and Dinnie was booked to go shopping with Kerry.

"Shopping?" he said, rather weakly, as she appeared at his door.

"Don't you like shopping?"

"I love it," said Dinnie, lying so convincingly that even Heather was moved to give him a firm nod of approval.

"Okay. Let's shop."

They went first to the psychedelic clothes shop in Ludlow Street. This had been a great success with Morag who, after visiting, had asked Kerry if she could possibly make her a fringed shoulder bag, a multicolored waistcoat, pink and red sunglasses, tartan tights and a headband with the Confederate flag on it. Kerry said she would do her best, and did. With Dinnie it was not such a success, but he pretended nobly.

Morag was meanwhile out with the Chinese fairies, searching for Magenta.

They laughed good-humoredly at her tales of Scotland and were sympathetic about her being forced to flee. They knew what it was like to be fugitives; back in China their families had suffered hard times, and the humans they had joined to cross the oceans had been fleeing from terrible oppression.

"Still," said Shau-Ju, "I do not understand why you did not simply hand back the pieces of the banner to the MacLeods right away. Then they would surely not have pursued you."

Morag shrugged, and said that the MacLeods were just not that reasonable.

Heather, now feeling fairly confident that Dinnie would not commit any outrages with Kerry, was settling into having a good time with the Italians. Her four prospective lovers showed her round the crowded streets of Little Italy, where the pavements outside the restaurants were jammed full of tables, and the quieter streets a few blocks north, where for some reason there was a series of shops selling guns.

Heather peered through the metal-clad windows and shuddered.

"If the MacLeods ever invent such things I'm done for."

"Why did you not simply hand back the pieces of the banner?" asked Cesare, but Heather could not give a convincing reason, save that the MacLeods were most unreasonable and would have chased them away.

Kerry took Dinnie to all her favorite clothes shops in the East Village. Afterwards they made their way home via the health food shop.

"He sure is a good-looking guy," said the assistants after they left.

"Looks like he's got a nice girl now."

The assistants were slightly disappointed in this.

"Got a nickel?" asked the beggar down the street.

Dinnie gave him five quarters, four nickels, and eight dimes, and apologized for not having any more change.

"No," said Morag. "I promise we are not the Persian cavalry. Nor are we hostile Carduchian tribesmen. Neither are we enemies from the country of the Drilae, or a force of Macrone warriors. We are not any of these things. We are Scottish and Chinese fairies."

"Ha, ha, ha," said Magenta. "Don't be ridiculous."

"Isn't it wonderful having fairies visiting us?" said Kerry.

"Truly wonderful," answered Dinnie, figuring that one more lie couldn't make a difference.

"But I'm sorry for Morag and Heather having to flee from Scotland."

Dinnie shrugged. He had never understood why they had not just given the pieces of the flag back, and said so to Kerry.

"Well," said Kerry. "I think the pieces have too much sentimental value for them. They can't bear to part with them."

"Sentimental value?"

"The bargaining did not go well," Morag informed Kerry, later in the evening. "Magenta refused utterly to give up the guitar, which we suspect of being Johnny Thunders' 1958 Gibson. However, after much hard negotiating, during which time she referred to me continually as an agent of Tissaphernes and threatened to set her Hoplites on me and to hell with the consequences, she eventually agreed to trade the Bhat Gwa mirror for a tin of shoe polish, a bottle of methylated spirits and a bag of assorted herbs and spices."

"And the Poppy?"

"She lost it."

Kerry was not surprised to hear this.

Heather rolled into Dinnie's rooms spectacularly drunk. It had taken her four attempts to mount the fire escape and a long time after that to climb in the window.

Dinnie was watching television. She lurched over him and clapped him heartily on the shoulder.

"Hey, Dinnie old buddy," she enthused. "These Italians certainly know how to show a girl a good time. How'd it go with Kerry?"

Dinnie seemed to shrink in his chair and did not reply.

"Well?"

"She stormed away in a bad mood. I don't think she wants to see me again," he replied finally.

Heather was aghast.

"But you were getting on so well. What went wrong?"

It took some time for Heather to drag the story out of him. Apparently Kerry had told Dinnie that she believed the reason Morag and Heather refused to let go of the fragments of the banner was because they had used them as blankets the first time they had had sex.

The sentimentality of this story left Kerry dewy-eyed. Unfortunately Dinnie had thrown back his head and guffawed heartily before saying he had always known they were a pair of goddamn lesbian pervert fairies and no wonder they had been chased out of Scotland. Probably they'd end up being chased out of the USA as well.

"And after that Kerry seemed to be upset."

Heather abused Dinnie for abusing Kerry's sensibilities in the strongest possible terms, for a very long time.

"You have now truly fucked the whole thing up. Good night."

THIRTY

Heather woke up with a sickening hangover. She tried to rise but could only make it to her hands and knees.

"My head feels as big as a tennis ball," she moaned, and crawled slowly along the carpet to the bathroom, her wings trailing down limply around her. She promised herself she would stick to Whisky in the future, and avoid wine completely.

Dinnie was woken up by a series of groans and gurgling noises.

"Good morning, Dinnie," said Heather, crawling back into his room. "I have just been sick in your shower stall."

"I hope you cleaned it up."

"I was too weak to reach the tap. Don't worry, fairy vomit is no doubt sweet-smelling to humans. Make me some coffee."

The thistle fairy was in a foul mood, partly because she was so hungover and partly because her hair was in such a state.

"The air here is filthy. It is ruining my looks."

"It helps if you don't crawl home in the gutter," commented Dinnie.

Heather sharply told him to shut up.

"If I'm going to think of a way for you to win your way back into Kerry's affections it will need total concentration. And let me say it is a difficult problem, enough to tax the mind of even a specialist like myself. Not only have you insulted

Kerry's friend Morag, you have insulted all her other friends who are lesbians by calling them perverts. Furthermore, you have mocked her for being sentimental and she will hate that.

"Worst of all, you let your true self shine through, and no woman is going to want to risk that happening a second time.

"It will require much thought. In other words, you keep your big mouth shut for the entire morning and leave me in peace."

Aelis and Aelric stood shoulder to shoulder, battling with Tala's mercenaries. Aelric had a sophisticated twin-sword-fighting technique and could hold his own even against the experienced mercenaries, as could Aelis, but the rebels were outnumbered and hard pressed.

After being surprised on a cattle raid they were now trying to reach the relative safety of Tintagel Castle.

Aelric slashed at his adversary, forcing him to retreat.

"I refuse to die without receiving a kiss from Marion," he moaned, breathing heavily.

"For the Goddess's sake," complained Aelis, "will you shut up about that bimbo and concentrate on fighting while I con- jure a mist."

Aelric and the others gathered around to Aelis to protect her while she magicked up a mist to help them escape.

Things were considerably more peaceful in Central Park now that Brannoc had made friends with the Ghanaian fairies. He had successfully explained who they were and where they came from and why, and apologized for any past misunder- standings.

The Ghanaians accepted these explanations and apologies

like the gracious folk they were, and now the three English and two Irish fairies were welcome to come and go as they pleased. Maeve, Padraig, Petal and Tulip were now frequent visitors in Harlem. Brannoc visited too, but his most favored destination was underneath a bush with his new girlfriend Ocarco, a fairy with black skin, black wings, black eyes, and an excellent gift for cheering up poor lonely homesick strangers.

Everyone was happy apart from Okailey, wise woman of the tribe. When she sniffed the air she did not like it. She could smell some strange scent coming from somewhere. There was a light breeze from the west which troubled her. Though they had dealt easily enough with the mercenaries, she did not think that their worries were over.

She told the park fairies of her forebodings and asked them to tell her everything they could about Tala, King of Cornwall.

"Do you really think he might invade?"

No one knew for sure but it seemed possible. His wizard, or technician a he now liked to be known, could send any amount of moonbows over the ocean if he wished, enough for an entire army.

There were one hundred and fifty Ghanaian fairies. Not enough to withstand such an invasion.

"What about the Italians and the Chinese?"

Okailey admitted that she did not know how many of them there were, but she doubted if either tribe numbered any more than hers. Living in the city parks did not seem to encourage much growth among their peoples. There was no room for their numbers to expand.

"I do not see how we could possibly match the numbers you say Tala can muster."

They contemplated the prospect of the entire English fairy host marching into Central Park. It was a grim thought.

"Well anyway," said Okailey, "we must decide what to do if it does happen. It may be that we shall just have to flee. But I think it would be as well to know what the other New York

fairies think. Normally we have no contact, but I have no decided to go to their territory and speak with them."

"It is odd," said Padraig, "that some fairies came here with
humans from Ghana, and from China, and from Italy, but none
seemed to have journeyed from Ireland. I know that many Irish
came to New York. I wonder why no Irish fairies accompanied
them?"

"Perhaps they could not be induced to leave the beautiful
green woods and meadows," suggested Maeve.

"Perhaps they were too drunk to get on the boat," suggested Brannoc.

"And what do you mean by that?" demanded Maeve bel-
ligerently. Okailey stopped the argument before it was started.
Her aura was both powerful and soothing and it was hard to
lose your temper in front of her.

She departed to make her arrangements for her journey
south to little Italy and Chinatown. Maeve, not pleased with
Brannoc's remark, announced that she was going to look for
some Irish fairies.

"If there are any more O'Briens here, we won't have to
worry about a Cornish army."

Heather spent the entire day either grumbling at Dinnie or trying to think of a way to win back Kerry's affections. When
Dinnie played his fiddle she abused his lack of skill, saying that
Morag was right, he was a disgrace to the MacKintoshes, and if
that tune was meant to be "De'il Amang the Tailors," then she
was a bowl of porridge.

When Dinnie listened to his tape of Bad Brains she said that
if he didn't like it, it was because the merits of the music were far
beyond the comprehension of his small brain and why didn't he
get on and practice his fiddle.

All in all, it was a tense day. Heather switched on the baseball and switched it off in frustration as the Yankee's manager came off worse in a fierce argument with the umpire. She moaned loudly about not being able to find a drop of proper malt whisky anywhere and more or less accused Dinnie of being personally responsible for the production of Jack Daniels.

She switched on the baseball again, just in time to see the Red Sox hit a home run.

"Oh, to hell with it. This is a bleak day. And I cannot think of what you should do next. You are an idiot, Dinnie, and you will never win Kerry now."

Dinnie slouched in his armchair, too depressed himself to reply to Heather's tirade of insults.

There was a knock on the door.

"Hello, Dinnie," said Kerry, flowers in her hair, bright smile on her face. "You want to come out with me tonight?"

After she left Heather was perplexed to the point of amazement. Was it possible that Dinnie had actually become so attractive that Kerry liked him even after his vile behavior?

"Ha, ha, you dumb elf," sniggered Dinnie. "So much for all your plans and worries. She wasn't insulted at all, she's practically beating the door down for another date."

"Yes, sir," Dinnie beamed at his mirror. "That girl recognizes a fine catch when she sees one."

Across the road Morag was struggling through the widow with a bag of candy and a beautiful yellow forsythia bloom.

"I couldn't have blamed you if you'd decided never to see him again," she said happily, and gave Kerry her presents.

"It's nothing," replied Kerry. "I promised to help you get the fiddle back, didn't I?"

Kerry was tired, and not very strong. so Morag went about the business of preserving the forsythia and fitting it into the alphabet. The flower alphabet, laid out on the floor surrounded by Kerry's favorite possessions, now looked so beautiful that it was bound to win the prize if it could only be completed.

THIRTY-ONE

Cesare, Luigi, Mario, Pierro and Benito sat with Heather in her favorite bar, perched on top of the TV. There was not a lot of room for six fairies even on a large television set, but the Italians were happy being close to Heather, although each wished that he were the only one. As each suitor for Heather was as keen as the next, finding a moment alone with her was proving to be impossible.

They drank whisky, which the Italians did not really like but tolerated because Heather promised they would soon acquire a taste for it. And when she apologized that the bar did not have a bottle of good Scottish malt, they said that they would see to it the next day, because their fairy family was good friends with the family who delivered drinks to the bar.

"Where have they gone on their date?" asked Mario, a pleasant, dark fairy who liked to show off his well-defined arm muscles.

"To a gallery in the West Village, then Kerry wants to do some shopping. They're going to eat at whatever restaurant takes their fancy, then on to a gig at the Thirteenth Street Squat."

"Sounds like a nice day."

Heather nodded. She was full of expectations for this day. If at the end of it Kerry were to throw her arms around Dinnie and declare love for him, or at least give him an appropriately passionate kiss, she would not at all be surprised.

It had been, she told her friends, a not inconsiderable feat.

"Of course he is a MacKintosh, which is a good start, but even so, if you'd seen that slob when I first took him in hand you would not have believed it was possible to make him attractive. But once we thistle fairies get on the case, the job's as good as done."

She bragged on happily like this for a while, and her suitors listened with intense interest, as suitors will.

Almost exactly paralleling this scene, at another bar a few blocks around Fourth Street, Morag sat with five young Chinese, drinking, laughing and awaiting the outcome of the day.

"As soon as that fool of a MacKintosh thinks Kerry's fallen in love with him, the MacPherson Fiddle will be mine by right."

They drank merrily in celebration, and the Chinese fairies told Morag that as well as being most beautiful she was extremely intelligent, as suitors will.

The MacLeod sisters sniffed the air as they walked along Seventeenth. Even here, with traffic fumes all around, it was clear to them all that there was a strange breeze blowing from the west. Mairi's second sight was clearing as she grew used to the city, but she could still not tell what it foretold.

She led them with a purpose nonetheless. She had a clear impression that at the end of this street they would find something interesting.

The four jagged-haired warriors arrived at Union Square.

"Well, Mairi," said Ailsa, "we've been here before and it looks no more interesting than last time."

She grimaced at the terrible roar from the far side of the square where a group of men seemed to be attacking the ground, pounding it with strange machines.

An enormous furniture delivery truck crawled its way down

Broadway and inched its way painfully round the road-works. Sitting on its roof were a group of twenty black fairies.

"Now that is interesting."

"Yes," agreed Kerry, sitting beside Dinnie in the cab home. "Hair dye can make a terrible mess. I once dyed my bath bright orange by accident and nothing would clean it off. Eventually I tried pissing on it at least once a day and after about a month it began to fade. Strong stuff, uric acid; you can break out of prison with it."

Kerry was a little drunk. It had been an enjoyable day. She had confidently led a dubious Dinnie into various expensive art galleries for a good look round, bought a yellow plastic necklace from a man selling junk from a suitcase just down from St. Mark's Place, had a not very successful attempt at eating a vegetarian meal in a Chinese restaurant and been highly pleased at the massed guitar noise at the gig.

Dinnie had got quite into the spirit of things, and had danced to the music without making a fool of himself. It was, he thought, the best day he had ever had.

The cab driver, a silent, morose man who did not abuse other drivers but stared fearfully at them through his windscreen, dropped them on East Fourth and grunted unhappily at Dinnie's large tip.

"Well, Dinnie, that was a good day. I am going to bed now because I am very drunk and sleepy. Come round tomorrow."

Kerry took hold of Dinnie's head, drew it down a little, and kissed him quite passionately, for quite a long time. She wandered off leaving Dinnie dazed on the sidewalk.

Up the road, perched on the sign above the bar, Heather and the Italians cheered.

"That's it," declared Heather, and swooped down on Dinnie's shoulder. "A passionate kiss, and she wants to see you tomorrow.

The fiddle is mine."

"Take it," said Dinnie, his eyes still glazed from the kiss. Heather and her friends flew and scrambled up the fire escape.

Farther down the road the kiss had also been observed by Morag and the Chinese.

"It worked," cried Morag, and the Chinese whooped with joy. Morag swept from her vantage point to clump down on Dinnie's shoulder.

She informed him that she had kept her promise and the fiddle now belonged to her.

"Fine," mumbled Dinnie, and Morag and her friends advanced up the steps of the theater.

Johnny Thunders sat on top of the theater building, musing on existence. Ostensibly, everything should be fine. After all, he had no more drug problems, he had Heaven to go back to . . . But his friends the Chinese fairies had told him that his Gibson Tiger Top was in the possession of a particularly demented bag lady and this spoiled everything. He felt the same dissatisfaction as he had once felt over the terrible mixes he seemed to be prone to on his records. Both New York Dolls albums and also the Heartbreakers album had been notorious for their poor sound quality. None of them was the magnificent work it should have been, given the great songs and his superb guitar technique.

Across the street lived Kerry, he knew. Should he ever get the chance he would show her a few things, although as he was now a spirit and inhabited a different domain, this would be difficult.

Okailey glanced up at the street sign.

"Fourth Street. We'll be in the territory of the Italians soon. Thank the Goddess. I will never ride down Broadway on a furniture truck again."

"Okailey," said one of her companions as they waited at the traffic lights.

"Yes?"

"There would seem to be fairies brawling in the street, just along the block."

Okailey and her companions looked on in astonishment.

"It's mine!" screamed Morag, and tugged at the fiddle.

"You stupid bitch of a MacPherson, it's mine," screamed Heather back at her. She was clutching the other end of the fiddle, which, as neither of them had yet had the time to shrink it down to fairy size, was much too heavy for either of them to make off with.

"I fulfilled the bargain!"

"What the hell d'you mean you fulfilled the bargain? You didn't have any bargain."

"Yes, I did," roared Morag. "I made Kerry fall in love with Dinnie."

"What?"

Heather, aware for the first time of the arrangement between her human companion and the foul MacPherson, was outraged.

"You disgusting backstabber, you've been interfering in my business again. How dare you sneak in and bargain with Dinnie. And anyway, it doesn't matter because I made the first bargain and it was me who made Kerry fall in love with him."

"What?" Morag was even more outraged on learning that Heather had dared to bargain the fiddle against the emotional well-being of her dear friend Kerry.

"How dare you bargain to make that nice Kerry fall in love with that scunner of a MacKintosh. It's monstrous. But it doesn't matter anyway because it was me who did it."

Morag was tempted here to announce that Kerry was only kidding anyway, but wisely refrained.

"It's mine!"

"It's mine!"

This was not a resolvable argument. Whoever's bargain had been the valid one, each of them was convinced that she had been responsible for its success. As their friends watched, the two thistle fairies shouted and raged at each other. After drinking all day they were both most excitable. Finally Heather, unable to control herself, slapped Morag's face.

Morag immediately let go of the fiddle and began trading punches with her opponent. They grappled with each other and rolled from the sidewalk into the gutter.

The Italians were alarmed. When Morag successfully landed a powerful kick in Heather's midriff, Mario felt he had to do something, and tried to restrain Morag's legs. The Chinese felt that this was hardly fair. Just as Heather managed to get her hands round Morag's throat, they rushed to their friend's aid. It then took no time at all for everyone to start fighting each other furiously.

And thus began the first street brawl of the New York fairies.

Aelis conjured up her mist and the rebels retreated in good order through a magic fairy space into the depths of Tintagel Castle. Once there, a furious argument broke out.

"How did they ambush us?" demanded Aelric's followers. "You personally went to scout out the ground and you assured us it was safe. What use is it burning Tala's warehouses and stealing his cattle if we all get killed?"

Aelric was hard pushed to find a reasonable explanation. The real reason he had failed to scout properly was that he had in fact been scouring the Cornish landscape for a triple-bloomed Welsh poppy to give Marion. His spy at the court had told him that she needed to complete her flower alphabet and would be so grateful to receive it that she would inevitably fall into his arms.

His mumbled apologies for the bungled mission were not well received, especially by fairies who had almost been killed in yet another futile effort to drop propaganda leaflets from the air.

Among any group of fairies there will be at least some limited telepathic powers, and in the fierce struggle cries for help went out so that in a very short time reinforcements from Chinatown to Little Italy were streaming into Fourth Street to join the mêlée.

"I can't believe it," said Okailey, striding regally along Fourth Street. "Fairies do not behave in this manner."

She strode up to Heather, still engaged in close combat with Morag.

"Stop this at once."

Heather unfortunately assumed that the hand on her should was of hostile origin and struck out wildly. Okailey's companions were stunned. They had never even imagined before that anyone could punch their revered sage in the face.

Dinnie eventually wandered back towards his room. His constant association with Heather had rendered him able to see all fairies, but he crossed the street in such a dream-like state that he did not notice the three tribes battling under his feet and around his head. The Chinese, Italians and Ghanaians were fighting on the ground and in the air, fluttering with swords and clubs from sidewalk to fire escape to lamp-post, screaming war cries and shouting for help.

Ailsa MacLeod watched from above in total incomprehension.

"You have brought us to something interesting, Mairi, but what?"

"Whatever it is, the MacKintosh and the MacPherson are right in the middle," said Rhona, pointing.

"And they are sore pressed," said Seónaid, slipping her dirk from its small sheath on her leg.

This posed a quandary for Ailsa. She did not want to see them killed before returning the pieces of the banner.

"And they are Scots," said Mairi, reading her mind.

It only took a few seconds' thought. The MacLeod fairies could not stand by and let fellow Scots clanswomen be destroyed by strangers, although among humans, clans had done much worse.

The sisters drew their weapons and swooped into the fray.

Kerry awoke, stretched lazily, and noticed that Morag was curled up beside her in bed. This was as normal, but today Morag was covered in cuts and bruises and her hair was sticky with blood.

Morag woke up, moaned and burst into tears.

"Tell me all about it," said Kerry soothingly, as she dangled the fairy over the sink to try to clean her cuts.

Morag, in deepest misery, told Kerry all about it. To Kerry it was a very surprising story. She could hardly believe that her pleasant friend had started a full-scale race war on the streets outside, and had a terrible picture of fairy police arriving with CS gas and riot shields to break things up.

"It was dreadful," said Morag. "Fighting everywhere, and me and Heather trying to kill each other, and strange fairies screaming and shouting and—"

She broke off to shudder.

"—and the MacLeods. Right in the middle of it, Ailsa MacLeod brandishing her claymore at me like the savage she is and screaming that once she'd saved me from the foreigners she was personally going to cut me into little pieces."

The MacLeods' arrival had, however, been fortunate for her and Heather. Well-armed, battle-hardened and disciplined, they had cleared a path through which the Scots had escaped to the side of the street, where they concealed themselves in a garbage can. By now very frightened by the chaos, Heather and Morag had stopped fighting each other and concentrated on hiding.

Morag winced as Kerry cleaned a wound on her scalp.

"What happened then?"

"The fighting went on a long time. Then the noise seemed to fade away. Eventually we looked out and there was no one around. Heather insulted me and I insulted her back but our hearts weren't in it. She went home and I came here."

"What about the MacLeods?"

Morag shrugged. They had been nowhere in sight. She didn't know why they had just left them. But the worst thing of all was the MacPherson fiddle. It was now lying smashed in the gutter, run over by a car.

"I have just destroyed my clan's greatest heirloom, one of the great fairy artifacts of Scotland."

Morag was utterly inconsolable, the most miserable fairy in New York by a long way—apart from Heather across the street, who was not feeling any better.

When Kerry finished cleaning and bandaging Morag she put her to bed and got on with the business of fitting her new colostomy bag for the day. She wondered what she could do to help. And she thought about her day out with Dinnie, which had been surprisingly enjoyable.

Johnny Thunders had been surprised to see fairies fighting on East Fourth Street. It reminded him of a riot at a gig one time in Sweden when he was so drunk he fell over on the stage and was unable to play.

The street was now quiet. He looked at the flower in his hands, dropped by Ailsa in the heat of battle. A very beautiful bloom, he thought.

THIRTY-TWO

Kerry was lying on cushions, tired and unwell. Today she had pains round her stomach which was always a worrying symptom. Nonetheless she was thinking about Morag's troubles.

"I really think you should hand back the pieces of the flag to the MacLeods. That at least would solve one problem."

"We can't." Morag shook her head.

"I know how you feel," said Kerry. "But aren't you taking sentiment too far? After all, you will still have the memory."

Morag looked puzzled and asked what Kerry was talking about. Kerry said she had guessed the reason the fairies would not give up their blankets.

Morag burst out laughing.

"That's not the reason we can't give the pieces back. The reason we can't give them back is because we used them to blow our noses on. It was a miserable cold night and we were both sniffly."

"You blew your noses on them?"

"That's right. And if the MacLeods ever find out that we used their revered Fairy Banner for handkerchiefs, there will be general warfare and carnage among Scotland's fairy population. The entire MacLeod clan would be over the water from Skye and marching on the MacPhersons and the MacKintoshes before you could blink."

"Really?"

"Really. I told you before that one thing you could not do to their banner was cut pieces off. Well, that is nothing compared to blowing your nose on it. A more deadly insult could not be imagined. Jean MacLeod, Queen of the Clan, would have the MacLeods of Glenelg, the MacLeods of Harris, the MacLeods of Dunvegan, the MacLeods of Lewis, the MacLeods of Waternish and the MacLeods of Assynt marching through the glens in a moment."

"There seem to be a lot of MacLeods."

"There is a terrible lot of MacLeods. And they'd bring their allies—the Lewises, the MacCrimmons, the Beatons, the Bethunes, the MacCraigs, the MacCaskills, the MacClures, the MacLures, the MacCorkindales, the MacCorquondales, the MacCuags, the Tolmise, the MacHarolds, the MacRailds, the Malcomsons, and probably a few more. There is a terrible lot of MacLeod allies as well.

"Attacking the MacPhersons and the MacKintoshes would raise the old fairy Clan Chattan confederation, provided they could stop feuding for a moment about who was in charge, and then the Davidsons, MacGillvrays, Farquarsons and Adamsons would come to our aid and there would be a terrible war. And if a war like that happens because Heather and I blew our noses on a flag, our lives won't be worth living."

Kerry considered this.

"How about washing it so they'll never know?"

"We tried. It can't be done. Nothing will remove the stains. One look at the pieces and Mairi MacLeod with the second sight will know."

Heather sat sadly at the bottom of the fire escape. She stared hopelessly down at the sidewalk, unable to imagine how things could be worse.

Dinnie, a fellow MacKintosh, had betrayed her, striking a secret bargain with a MacPherson. Ashamed of her clan, she shuddered.

The MacPherson Fiddle was smashed. First the MacLeod Banner, then the MacPherson Fiddle. Thank the Goddess the MacKintosh Sword was still in Scotland or she might have broken that as well. Important clan heirlooms just seemed to crumble in her hands.

Neither she nor Morag would ever be able to go home again, and as they were now bitter enemies, they would both be on their own.

And then there were the MacLeods. Where had they gone? It hardly mattered. There was no longer any possibility of flight. Once Mairi MacLeod had your scent, there was no escape.

Heather felt that she hardly cared. She put her finger through a hole in her kilt, which had re-opened despite her attempt to patch it with Dinnie's cushion cover. For a fairy, Heather was extremely bad at mending.

Behind her, Titania ran through her lines.

"You stupid scunner!" exploded Heather, materializing suddenly. "That's not how a fairy queen would talk!"

Titania panicked and ran from the theater.

"Well, Kerry, I have just been up on the rooftops talking with Johnny Thunders and there is some good news and some bad news."

Kerry looked up from the beads she was stringing.

"The good news is that he has told me every note in the guitar break on 'Vietnamese Baby,' which I will now be able to teach you, providing the MacLeods let me live long enough. The bad news is that he found the poppy after the battle outside and gave it to the Chinese fairies to trade with Magenta for the guitar. It has slipped through our grasp again."

Kerry wailed.

Morag scratched her head, slightly itchy from too much hair dye.

"When the Chinese brought him the guitar it wasn't his old Gibson after all. It was a cheap Japanese copy. He's really annoyed."

So was Kerry. The way this woman Magenta kept making off with her prize flower was infuriating beyond belief.

Morag found Heather sitting on the steps, still chuckling about the fleeing Titania.

"Give me your piece of the banner."

"What?"

"Give me your piece of the banner and don't argue about it."

Heather shrugged, unwrapped her fiddle and handed the green cloth to Morag. Morag flew back across the road to Kerry's. She reappeared moments late and rejoined Heather, but before she could speak, Ailsa, Seónaid, Mairi and Rhona MacLeod—cut and bruised, but still glowing with health— landed gracefully beside them.

"Let's talk," said Ailsa, and unslung her claymore.

Heather and Morag slumped in resignation.

The MacLeods had been distracted in the battle by the arrival of the still rampaging Cu Sidth dog which, attracted by the fairies, had raced down Fourth Street and attacked Rhona. No sooner had they driven it away and killed it than they found themselves surrounded by unknown tribes. Fortunately the regal Okailey had then managed to halt the fighting.

"The New York tribes have gone their various ways," said Ailsa. "But they are hostile and suspicious of each other.

Thanks to you pair, I understand. You have a talent for upsetting people."

"How did the famous MacPherson Fiddle come to be in New York? Mairi recognized it before it was broken," said Rhona.

Heather and Morag admitted they did not know. Nor did anyone know where the pieces had got to.

Seónaid fingered her dirk.

"Where are the fragments you cut from our banner?"

Four Puerto Ricans appeared in the corner with their tennis ball and tried keeping it in the air with their heads. They took up the whole sidewalk so passers-by had to make their way past on the road. The passers-by included a man taking a weasel for a walk on a leash. This made the MacLeods stare, but not Heather and Morag because they had seen it before.

Heather was at a complete loss. She knew what was going to happen when she handed back her piece of cloth. Mairi would take one look at it and know it had been used as a handkerchief. Death would arrive immediately after, followed by a raising of the clans back home.

"Why," said Morag brightly, "we have the pieces safely with us. We are really very sorry we cut them from your banner—it was an accident and we did not know what we were doing. Come with us and we'll give them to you."

She led the way across the road.

"Are you mad?" hissed Heather. "You know what's going to happen now."

"Trust me," whispered Morag.

"Hello," said Kerry brightly as they appeared. "You must be the MacLeods I've been hearing about. You are even more gracious and lovely than Morag and Heather's descriptions of you. Would you like some tea?"

"No."

"Are you sure? Morag has taught me how to make a good Scottish cup of tea."

"The banner."

"Right."

Kerry opened a drawer and took out two clean bits of cloth, handing them to Ailsa.

"As you can see," said Kerry. "Morag and Heather have treated them with great respect."

Mairi sniffed at them. She pronounced them undamaged.

"And perhaps they may yet be sewed back on to the banner with no harm done."

"We would have given them back before," said Morag, "only you never gave us a chance to explain."

"I still have a mind to cut you to pieces."

"Right," said Morag." But before you do, consider this. I see your sporran was cut and ripped during the fight. And, with one of these psychic insights which I am so well known for, I have a strong feeling that your sporran held all your fairy magic, namely your sleep spells, and your means of returning home. Is this not true?"

Ailsa admitted that it was. Her spell for magicking a moon-bow back to Scotland was gone, lost on the winds of the Lower East Side.

"But we still have one," lied Morag. "Just let bygones be bygones, and we can all go home together."

"I know a rich merchant who lives in these parts," Magenta told her men. "We will trade with him."

Her force had now passed through the dangerous mountains to the north of Persia and reached the coast. The coast was occupied partly by Greeks, which was an improvement, although even fellow Greeks were not necessarily going to be pleased to see a force of lawless and battle—hardened mercenaries camped outside their walls.

What they needed now were ships to make their last part of

the journey home easier. Xenophon would trade some of her booty with the merchant.

In his shop on Canal Street, Hwui-Yin was not displeased to see Magenta. Often in the past they had had interesting talks when the grey-haired lady had brought him something to sell.

"Why do you give her money for such rubbish?" asked his assistant after she left, and Hwui-Yin explained that he was always sympathetic to a bag lady with a sound knowledge of classical Greece.

"If she wants to sell me a broken child's fiddle to buy boot polish, why not? At least I get a good explanation of why the Athenians found it necessary to execute Socrates."

Kerry, a persistent host, got the MacLeods to accept some tea, oatcakes and honey. After their hardships, they were not averse to a spell of comfort.

"How did you manage it," whispered Heather.

"Kerry did it," whispered Morag in reply. "With modern washing technology. She just shoogled the bits round in her machine for a wee while and they came out fine. Apparently washing is more advanced here than in Cruickshank. They have special powders for washing even the most delicate fabric at a low temperature and making it completely clean. And also something called fabric conditioner which makes it soft, pleasant and good as new."

Heather was impressed.

"There are certainly many good things in New York," she said, immensely relieved.

THIRTY-THREE

Disaster threatened from all corners. The Italian, Chinese and Ghanaian fairies had retreated to their home territories but remained alert to the possibility of war. The forces of Tala the King were ready to invade New York, while his special mercenary band had surrounded Aelric in Tintagel Castle.

Dinnie, unaided by Heather's bank robberies, was facing imminent eviction; and Heather, outraged at the treachery of his bargain with Morag, would not lift a finger to help. The MacLeod fairies were for the moment pacified, but still talked of taking Heather and Morag home to Skye to stand trial for theft. Meanwhile they would not let them out of their sight.

"And the MacPherson Fiddle is smashed," groaned Heather, gloomily sharing a dram with Morag in the bar on the corner. They had themselves settled down into a moody truce. As to whose the fiddle would have been had it still existed, the Goddess only knew. If Kerry really had fallen in love with Dinnie it would have been Heather's; if she had only been pretending it would have been Morag's. Kerry herself was being reticent.

Morag had only wanted Kerry to pretend, but the fairy was not sure any more. She suspected that Kerry had enjoyed herself too much on her last date.

If Kerry had really fallen for Dinnie she was not letting on, but Morag wondered if this might be to avoid upsetting her. After all, if Kerry really did love Dinnie, the fiddle would have been Heather's by right.

By popular vote Aelric was deposed as rebel leader, accused of spending too much time dreaming about the King's stepdaughter.

"A bit less dreaming and a bit more planning and we might not be trapped in Tintagel Castle."

Their situation was bad. Inside the ruins of the castle the rebels had few supplies and were fast growing hungry. Outside, the forty-two mercenaries, now reunited, patrolled the perimeter and flew overhead, kept out only by Aelis' fast-weakening spell of mystification. If any mercenary tried to set foot in the castle he suddenly and quite uncontrollably found himself heading in the wrong direction, ending up confused and dizzy and back where he started. But the mercenaries, being fairies, understood this sort of spell and knew Aelis could not keep it up for long, particularly if she had no food.

Werferth sent a message to the King telling him that the rebellion would soon be at an end.

Heather and Morag sat on top of the sign over a gun shop, glowering at each other. Heather proclaimed loudly that it was not her fault.

"Yes it is," retorted Morag. "You and your hopeless addiction to flirting with any fairy not actually certified dead."

They had met Magenta outside the bar. She admitted she had the poppy from Johnny Thunders via the Chinese fairies, but claimed that after taking it out to admire it on Spring Street she had been approached by a winged Roman soldier who asked if he could trade her for the flower, as he knew it would

be a perfect gift for a blonde Caledonian girl he was in love
with. He had paid Magenta a good price, and departed.

"In other words," Morag sneered at Heather, "some Italian
fairy now has the poppy as a means of getting underneath your
kilt. Honestly, Heather, the trouble your sex drive has cost us
over the years is just ridiculous."

"Well, what about you and the Chinese fairies?" retorted
Heather.

"They are all fairies of great good taste," sniffed Morag,
"and would not rob a sick young woman of a vital flower merely as a ploy for bedding a well-respected visitor from
Scotland."

Heather sniffed back at her. "Well, anyway. All I have to do
is wait for Cesare or Luigi to arrive and give me the flower.
Then Kerry can have it back."

Brannoc was horrified to learn of the incident on East Fourth
Street, particularly the part where Heather punched Okailey in
the mouth. Apparently Okailey would not have minded so
much except she was being carried along the street by the tide
of battle and couldn't get in a good blow in return.

"Well, our problems are solved," announced Maeve, fluttering down to join them.

"You found some Irish fairies?" said Padraig eagerly.

"No," admitted Maeve, "I didn't. I don't know why, but
there don't seem to be any on this island."

"I think the Irish communities are probably in Brooklyn or
the Bronx," suggested Ocarco.

"Possibly. I have not had time to hunt in foreign countries.
Anyway, it doesn't matter. I have written to my clan asking
them to come over the water."

Brannoc looked perplexed.

"You've done what?"

A young couple seeking peace caused a rare disturbance in the clearing, wandering in with two bottles of beer and an anchovy pizza, and forcing the fairies to withdraw into the bushes.

"I've written to them. I've just posted the letter and they should be here in a few days."

Brannoc's wings shook with laughter.

"That's the most stupid thing I've ever heard. How is your letter going to get there? You can't send a letter to fairies through the humans' postal system."

Maeve was indignant.

"You might not be able to in England, but you can in Ireland. The Irish have great respect for their fairies. I addressed it to the O'Brien fairies, just South of Grian Mach, Brugh na Boinne. It will get there fine, you'll see."

Disgusted with this piece of stupidity on Maeve's part, Brannoc departed with Ocarca to make love in a tree-top, as a change from under a bush.

He heard from a squirrel who heard from a sparrow who heard from a seagull who heard from an albatross that the Cornish troops were almost ready to march, and apart from making love while there was still time, he could think of nothing else to do.

"Will the English troops trouble us?" asked Aba, up in Harlem, "or will they leave us alone if they capture Petal and Tulip?"

"I doubt they will leave us alone," said Okailey. "Once these imperialists reach your country, they never go."

Cesare flew smartly up to the gun-shop sign.

"Heather, I have a present for you."

He handed over a flagon of whisky and a pouch full of magic mushrooms.

"Where's the poppy?"

"The poppy? I traded it to some Chinese fairy for these. He wanted it for some girl he's met. I thought you'd like them better."

Heather moaned and covered her eyes with her wings. Morag batted Cesare down off the sign and flew home in disgust.

Dinnie was mightily disgusted. He was being forced to quit his apartment and Heather flatly refused to help, saying that she would not procure money for a traitor to the clan.

With only nine dollars left in the world Dinnie did the only thing possible, and went to buy some beer.

"Things are not so bad, Kerry. I expect a Chinese fairy to bring me the poppy any minute. I understand he is fatally attracted to me and will do anything to please me."

Kerry was joyful at this news, although not at much else. The judging was only a few days away and she was not feeling well enough to carry on. Her insides hurt and diarrhea flowed into her colostomy bag.

Morag had been keen to ask about her feelings for Dinnie, but in view of Kerry's poor state of health, she let it pass.

Morag had had one very unsatisfactory discussion about the matter with the MacLeods.

"Whoever the fiddle belongs to, you are not the best fiddler in Scotland," declared Ailsa. "Everyone knows that the best young fiddler in Scotland is Wee Maggie MacGowan. She would have won the junior fiddling contest no bother if she hadn't been down with the measles that week."

"Wee Maggie MacGowan?" Morag was outraged at the

suggestion. "She is nothing but a wee clipe, always telling tales on people and cooeying up to her fiddle teacher."

"None the less, she is the best fiddler."

This just went to prove how weak-brained the MacLeods were. Wee Maggie MacGowan indeed!

Kerry, despite her poor state of health, selected a new mirror-studded waistcoat and made to leave, saying that she felt like a breath of fresh air.

Morag, well known for her psychic insights, followed silently.

THIRTY-FOUR

Aelis met a thoughtful-looking Aelric at the bottom of a ruined turret. He had been out scouting for some secret means of escape.

"Well?"

Aelric shook his head.

"No sign of a triple-bloomed poppy anywhere."

Aelis fluttered her wings in frustration.

"You were meant to be looking for a way out. My spell will last for approximately one hour longer."

"Right," said Aelric. "A way out. I forgot about that. Let me think for a while."

Heather and Morag sat on the railing of a tiny park on Fourteenth Street, discussing how bad things were. This was a popular occupation for fairies these days.

Four young prostitutes were arranged along the sidewalk.

"Only twenty dollars," they said to men passing by. "I'll stay a long time. Only twenty dollars."

Business did not seem to be good and the prostitutes slouched dejectedly against the railings.

From any point of view the affair of Dinnie and Kerry had gone disastrously wrong. Morag, following Kerry across the street, had found Dinnie naked on the floor with the assistant from the health food shop. Kerry was not pleased and now lay unhappily on cushions playing her guitar.

Dinnie protested to the disgusted Heather that it was all a mistake and he still really loved Kerry, but the fairy, after a few cutting insults concerning his sexual performance and what an unimpressive sight he made in the shower, had simply packed her things and left.

"I did not spend all that time making you attractive to Kerry for you to fuck the first person to show any interest."

A Chinese fairy called Shau-Ju had later appeared with a present for Morag.

"At last," breathed Morag, nudging Kerry. "The poppy."

Shau-Ju produced a flagon of whisky from his bag and some magic mushrooms. When questioned by a less than pleased Morag, he protested hotly that it was not his fault he no longer had the poppy. Four Italian fairies led by Cesare had robbed him of it on the way here. Back home, Shau-Ju's kin were already strapping their swords.

"We started another race war," moaned Morag.

"One more probably won't hurt," said Heather.

"Fine," said Kerry, crossly. "You all just have fun with the damn thing. Don't mind me."

Heather and Morag thought that really it was not their fault if they were so irresistible that other fairies committed crimes to bring them presents, but did not say so to Kerry.

Later that evening Mairi, who as far as they were concerned had far too many second sights for her own good, had prophesied that any time now a vast army of evil Cornish fairies would descend on New York.

"Looking for Petal and Tulip, I suppose," said Heather, eyeing the prostitutes.

"I wonder what happened to them? We haven't seen any sign of them since you got us all separated."

Petal and Tulip rode down Fourteenth Street on a 1938 Buick.
"We found you!" they exclaimed, fluttering over to the railings.

Johnny Thunders was on the verge of giving up. He had hunted all
of New York and nowhere was there any trace of a 1958 Gibson
Tiger Top. And yet . . . he was continually drawn back to East
Fourth Street. There was something about this place, something
vaguely familiar. If he concentrated he could almost feel the presence of his guitar.

"Is that really suitable music for the court of Theseus, King of
Athens" queried an actor in the theater.

Cal looked down at his guitar.

"Course it is," he replied. "Why not?"

He waved away the objection. With only three days till the
staging of *A Midsummer Night's Dream* and his Titania still in a state
of shock, he was in no mood to listen to complaints about his stage
music.

Tulip still had a little difficulty adjusting to Morag's appearance.
He had not seen anything quite like it since the last Glastonbury
festival in England, and even the young and old hippies he saw
there were not quite as bright. Heather, after one day at Kerry's,
was not far behind, and when she moved now the bells at the bottom of her kilt jingled merrily.

The explanations about what had been going on that flowed
between the four were very confusing, but after they had made
some sort of sense of it Petal and Tulip explained that with the
English army ready to cross the Atlantic, New York's fairies must
put aside their arguments and present a united defense.

"Otherwise there is no hope at all. We know all about the fight
in your street. Brannoc and Ocarco and Okailey are furious. But

even so, we are going to see the Italians and the Chinese and try to mend things."

"That might be difficult," said Heather and Morag in unison. "Try and avoid personal relationships."

Aelis could no longer maintain her spell of mystification. Tintagel Castle lay open to invasion. Outside, mercenaries' dogs sensed this and howled. The twenty-five rebels huddled miserably underneath the castle, in the cavern men called Merlin's Cave. They were hungry and in rags.

"So much for the peasants' revolution."

Aelric lifted his head.

"Of course. I remember. Something I read in the library about Chairman Mao. He one time saved the day with a very long swim."

"And?"

"We will swim our way out of here," declared Aelric, a little of his former spirit returning. "Find a river. Failing that, a well."

The two Scots fairies took Petal and Tulip to Kerry's apartment. When they explained their mission, Ailsa was skeptical.

"How are you going to reconcile the warring tribes?"

Petal and Tulip did not exactly know, but claimed to have some skills of diplomacy, as their father was a king.

"You could try being cute and appealing," suggested Heather. "Always works for me."

"Could you bring help from Scotland?" asked Tulip, relating the tale of Maeve and the letter. Neither Heather nor Morag thought this would work for them.

"The village postman in Cruickshank is awful grumpy these days. Everyone keeps blaming him for the price of stamps going up. I wouldn't trust him to deliver a letter to the fairies."

"It's no problem," declared Ailsa. "You have the means of magicking a moonbow home, don't you? We'll just go and get help."

Heather and Morag made a hasty exit, saying that they felt it was their duty to introduce Petal and Tulip to the Chinese and Italians, and also see if they could find Kerry's flower.

"Now you've got us into another mess with your lies and stories," complained Heather, a complaint which was naturally developed into a full-blown argument as to which clan was most likely to bribe the judges at a junior fiddling contest, the MacKintoshes or the MacPhersons, and could easily have led to blows.

"You were meant to be introducing us to the Italians and Chinese."

A hideous noise emanated from across the street.

"Ha, ha," chortled Morag. "Dinnie's got his old fiddle out. There's a MacKintosh—playing for you."

"Nothing to do with me," replied Heather, hotly. "I don't believe he really is a MacKintosh at all."

Upstairs, Dinnie had dredged up the old fiddle he had played at school, and was trying to remember the tunes he'd learned.

I'll show that ignorant bitch of a fairy, he thought to himself. I'll earn my rent busking. No one is going to evict Dinnie MacKintosh without a struggle.

"What an amazing upturn in business," said one of the young prostitutes to her friend back on Fourteenth Street. "I never saw so many eager clients before."

Both she and her friends were doing a roaring trade, and had been ever since the fairies had perched behind them, because there is nothing like the aura of a group of fairies for spreading sexual desire.

THIRTY-FIVE

It was dusk and in Central Park Padraig and Maeve were just warming up on the pipes and fiddle, running gently through 'The Queen of the Fairies,' an air which the famous blind harpist O'Carolan learned from the Irish fairies. They moved through some sedate renditions of hornpipes and slip jigs before breaking into a fierce version of 'McMahon's Reel,' and 'Trim the Velvet.'

While Maeve took a brief break to tune her pipes Padraig played his customary version of 'Banish Misfortune.'

"Now what misfortune would you be suffering from, over here on a fine adventure in a new country?" called a voice from far above.

Out of a thin cloud a moonbow of seven shades of green was falling to the ground on it, marching cheerfully, were around two hundred fairies.

"Well, here are the O'Briens, and some others," said the female fairy at their head, stepping on to the ground. "We got your letter. What trouble have you been getting yourself into now, Maeve O'Brien?"

"It is truly wonderful what reasonable creatures we fairies are," Morag informed Kerry. "Only the other day three tribes were fighting and battling on the street outside and now, thanks to a few honest words from Petal and Tulip, everything is all right again. Peace reigns everywhere."

"Apart," Kerry pointed out, "from the vast and well-armed Cornish army which is heading our way."

"Yes, apart from that. Although I'm sure most of them are reasonable too. They are just under the thrall of an evil King."

"Much like the United States."

"And now that the streets are safe, I am off to see Cesare. I will be back with your flower in no time."

Kerry was tired. In the privacy of her toilet she had discovered that some blood had trickled from her anus. This always happened when she overdid things and roused the disease in her intestines into activity. It was a frequent and distressing reminder of her illness which always made her depressed, no matter how often it happened. With the strain of the Community Arts Prize coming up, Kerry had been feeling unwell more and more frequently. She lay down to sleep, leaving the MacLeods to have words with Heather.

"Mairi tells me that you two do not in fact have the ability to make a moonbow between here and Scotland."

"And how does she know that?" demanded Heather.

"She has the sight."

Heather sighed. Mairi's powerful second sight was a terrible nuisance. It was practically impossible to deceive her in anyway.

"And this lie is a further insult by you to the MacLeods," continued Ailsa, her black eyes boring into Heather. "But I shall overlook that for the moment because there are other matters more important. We are of the opinion that all Scottish fairydom is in danger from the Cornish King. If he succeeds in dominating this place there will be no stopping them. Mairi had a vision of his army marching through the borders and right up to the Highlands. This we cannot allow." Ailsa tilted her spiked hair towards her sister. "Mairi has sent a message to Scotland for help."

"How?"

"She has sent a vision of our plight over the water. The Scots will march over a moonbow of their own, and you will guide them down in the correct place by playing, 'Tullochgorum' at the appropriate moment."

Morag crawled wearily up the fire escape, worn out by recent events. She was pleased to find Kerry sleeping, although it only delayed telling her the bad news about Cesare being so hospitable to Petal and Tulip that he was moved to give them the poppy as a present, and Petal and Tulip subsequently feeling sorry for a miserable woman they met on the sidewalk that they in turn were moved to give it to her.

"It is such a powerful and beautiful flower," explained Petal.

"We knew it would cheer her up. And we are good fairies," explained Tulip.

"You are morons," growled Morag.

THIRTY-SIX

A elric and his followers swam for their lives down a secret well in Merlin's Cave and into a cold underground stream, emerging on Bodmin Moor only half alive, but safe.

"Good plan, Aelric." Aelis weakly tried to shake water from her sodden wings.

A damp breeze blew over the moor.

"What's that?"

Nearby was a circle of standing stones. Rising from the stones was a series of moonbows, and behind them was gathered the full host of Tala's army.

Dinnie did not know what to do about Kerry. He could understand that she would not have been pleased to find him having sex with a casual acquaintance but, never having been in this position before, he was at a loss as to how to rectify things.

"So who gives a shit anyway?" he demanded out loud to his empty room. "I never liked her anyway. She is a bimbo. Almost as stupid as that dumb asshole of a fairy."

He was finished with fairies. He did not ever want to see one again. He did not need them to run his love life. Nor did he need them to pay his rent. He would busk. Armed with his old fiddle and his new repertoire of tunes, he was confident of success.

Outside it was hot and clammy, which made Dinnie desire an immediate beer. He headed for the deli. By the theater's steps, a tramp's dead body was being loaded into an ambulance. Dinnie was so used to it by now he hardly glanced at it.

"Don't you shithead fairies have anything to do than hang around on doorsteps all day?" he said loudly, and strode past.

"Aren't you going to visit Kerry?" asked Morag.

Dinnie snorted derisively.

"Who needs her? Plenty of women have got their eye out on me these days, I can tell you."

"Well, he seems to be returning to normal," said Morag, and Heather agreed.

"Bit of a relief really. A polite Dinnie was hard to take."

"Is Kerry sad about it?"

"I don't know."

Dinnie made his way to Washington Square and made ready to play. After two beers and a packet of cookies he was full of confidence. When a stray dog ran up to him he had no hesitation in dealing it a sound kick in the ribs, sending it away hurt and confused. He tucked his fiddle under his now finely contoured chin and started to play. On this hot day the park was full, an ideal opportunity to earn his rent.

Just then a girl who very much looked like Kerry walked past and he found himself severely distracted. His arm shook a little. A slight pain gnawed at his heart.

He lowered his fiddle and hurried away for more beer.

"Where is this moonbow taking us?"

Sheilagh MacPherson, Chief of the Clan, shrugged her shoulders. It was crossing the Atlantic but what was on the other side of the Atlantic, she was unsure. Unlike some of her clan she never spent time in public libraries looking at human books.

"Wherever it is taking us, we will know when we get there, because the MacLeod sisters will guide us in with a version of 'Tullochgorum.'"

"And wherever we end up, I am sure Morag MacPherson will be on the end of it. I will be pleased to have her back safe, providing she refrains from starting any more trouble with the Macleods. It is a wonder we are all marching here together at all, and only a sign of how serious things are."

Behind the MacPherson clan came the MacKintoshes and behind hem came the MacLeods and their confederates. The message from Mairi, Scotland's most powerful seer and sender, had come not only to them in Skye but had traveled on past the Wester Isles into the heartland of Scotland. Now the whole of the Clan Chattan confederation had joined the MacLeods on the march to New York.

It was no surprise to any of the clan chiefs that trouble was brewing with King Tala. According to the wise among them, it had only ever been a matter of time before this happened.

"As his industrial society expands, he will have to seek new markets abroad," said Glen MacPherson, a studious young fairy who did spend a fair amount of time in libraries. "What's more, to gather in the raw materials he needs at suitably low prices, he will have to conquer these markets by force. A policy of imperialist expansion is inevitable."

"And what does that mean?" asked Sheilagh MacPherson.

"It means he'll attack us."

Sheilagh snorted.

"We need not worry about that. Once we have the MacPherson fiddle in our hands, no one can attack us."

Agnes MacKintosh, Clan Chief, carried the famous MacKintosh sword, a renowned weapon made by the fairies for Viscount Dundee. With the prospect of the recovery of the MacPherson Fiddle and the repair of the MacLeod Banner, there was good reason for optimism, for any army carrying these three powerful icons could not be defeated.

Underneath, the Atlantic was vast and gray but over the moonbow progress was swift.

Three beers later, Dinnie felt he was ready to play. The strange feeling inside had subsided. This was just as well. It was ruinous to his finances.

Deciding that to make some quick money an impressive tune was called for, Dinnie once more leveled his violin. To his great dissatisfaction he noticed that none of the crowd in Washington Square was actually looking his way, being busy either sleeping in the sun or shouting encouragement to the numerous junior baseballers who were pitching, hitting, and striking out in various parts of the park. A complete waste of time, as far as Dinnie could see.

A young woman who looked remarkably like Kerry walked her dog right in front of him and his bow made a painful scraping noise as it slid down the neck of his violin.

"Go walk your dog somewhere else," he bawled. "I'm trying to play some music here."

"Is that what it was?" answered the girl brightly, and strolled off. From behind she still looked like Kerry.

Dinnie found himself shaking again. He hurried off for more beer.

Heather, Morag and the MacLeods sat on top of the theater.

"Right," called Mairi. "I can sense the Scots are approaching. Guide them in."

"No problem," answered Heather, scooping her fiddle out if its bag and under her chin. "One expert version of 'Tullochgorum' coming up."

Morag gaped.

"What? You are going to play it? Your playing of 'Tullochgorum' will probably send them into the Hudson River. I'll do it." Morag whipped out her own fiddle.

Heather was outraged.

"You stupid besom, you can't play 'Tullochgorum' to save your life. I'll play it."

"No, I'll play it."

Ailsa had a strong desire to strangle them both.

"Will one of you just hurry up and play the damned thing before the Scots army overshoots."

"Well," said Heather, rounding on her. "If you MacLeods spent a bit less time practicing with claymores and a bit more learning the fiddle, maybe you could play it. But you can't, so there. I'm going to do it."

"You are not. I'll do it."

Morag started up the playing, Heather grabbed her fiddle, and they started to fight.

Rhona, Seónaid and Mairi tried to separate the screaming pair. Ailsa just hung her head and wished she was back on the island of Skye, where the fairies were neither psychedelically dressed nor feeble brained.

Kerry, finding her apartment unusually empty of fairies, took the opportunity to lay out her flower alphabet, staring lovingly at her latest addition, a bright-yellow bloom of *Rhododendron campylocarpum*. This completed the alphabet, apart from the Welsh poppy.

On display, the thirty-two blooms, preserved as if fresh with loving care, were a soothing and beautiful sight.

Kerry was pleased to have got so far, although the lack of the poppy meant it was incomplete and she could not win the prize. She could not enter her alphabet incomplete. It would offend her artistic sensibilities too much. Botticelli would not

have painted half a fresco in the Sistine Chapel. Neither would
Johnny Thunders have put down half a guitar solo on record.

It seemed unfair though. A man who had deserted her after
promising to teach her how to play guitar did not deserve to
win public acclaim.

Cal deserves a punch in the mouth, thought Kerry. And if I
ever get strong I will give him one.

She sighed, and made ready for a trip to the drugstore.
Every few weeks she had to pick up a large prescription of
colostomy bags and the assorted bits and pieces that held them
on, cleaned the hole in her side, and so forth, along with a supply of steroids to suppress the disease.

She no longer believed that she would ever get a reversal
operation, and the thought of having the bag forever was more
depressing than she could bear.

She was tired. It seemed like a long time since she had been
really healthy.

As the rebels watched, the English army marched from the
standing stones up the moonbows. Mercenary dogs howled in
the distance.

"They're on to us!"

The rebels' wings dropped in despair. After days of hunger
and an exhausting underground swim they could not outdis-
tance their pursuers on Bodmin Moor.

"The moonbows!" cried Aelric. "We will sneak up into the
sky once the army is out of sight."

The others stared as him, amazed by his audacity. Surely
their former leader was returning to his previous brilliant
ways.

Aelric had in fact noticed Marion going up the moonbow
with a sword strapped to her side, and wherever she was
going, he was keen to follow.

While on Heather's health regimen, Dinnie had only been allowed one beer a day. Now, after nine cans of Schlitz, his emotional turmoil has quieted but his violin technique was abominable. He struggled to get his fingers round the notes but it was no use. Hearing his atrocious efforts, people's attention was drawn away from the baseball and the sleepers woke, but only to abuse him and demand that he cease immediately.

"How dare you insult me," bawled Dinnie defiantly. "You ought to be grateful to hear a fine rendition of 'Tullochgorum.'"

"Well, is that what is was?" said Sheilagh MacPherson, Chief of the Clan, landing gently beside him. "We weren't sure. We though perhaps a Scottish fiddler was under attack and using her fiddle to beat off the enemy. Still, thanks for guiding us down. Where are Heather an Morag?"

Dinnie looked up and groaned. Stretching way up into the sky and apparently visible only to him, a vast array of kilted fairies were marching groundwards.

"Why me?" he mumbled. "I'm just a normal guy. I don't deserve this."

THIRTY-SEVEN

The moon shone on Central Park. A series of moonbows slid out of the sky and down the moonbows came the English fairy host, row upon row.

The fairies below stared in horror at the enormity of Tala's force. Regiment after regiment marched swiftly to the ground, heavily armed fairies and all manner of evil looking kindred spirits and Cu Sidth dogs by their side.

"We're done for," whispered Tulip, and beside her Okailey, Shau-Ju and Cesare nodded agreement. It seemed like New York's fairies had made up their differences only in time to be slaughtered by a savage invasion force.

"Where are the Scots?" they enquired urgently of Rhona and Seónaid MacLeod, who had been sent up as representatives from East Fourth Street. The MacLeods did not know. Though they should have crossed the water by now, the clans had not arrived.

"Never mind," said Maeve, and slapped the backs of a few of her Irish comrades. "We'll see them off."

The Irish muttered in agreement, but none of them except Maeve was convinced.

After her further argument with Morag, Heather sat on Johnny

Thunders' knee on the corner of East Fourth and Bowery. They had just met, although Heather knew from Morag about the dissatisfied guitarist's hunt for his Tiger Top.

Johnny nodded down the Bowery, to where CBGB's was, and told Heather about some good times he had had playing there.

"I guess I should be getting back to Heaven soon," he sad. "The Festival of Hungry Ghosts must be drawing to a close, and I wouldn't want to be left out."

Magenta strolled up to them, looking strong and fit. After her recent meetings with fairies and her large intake of Fitzroy cocktail, she had no difficulty in seeing creatures invisible to the rest of the world.

Seemingly free from Persian pursuit and jealous attacks from other Greeks, she sat down for a talk, and the many and various experiences the three of them had had recently made for a very interesting conversation indeed.

In doorways a little way down the street, down-and-outs were doing likewise, just sitting and talking, with nothing much else to do.

"Thanks, Magenta," said Johnny, accepting a drink. "A little strong on boot polish maybe, but not bad." He fingered the broken old guitar that he had mistakenly traded with the bag lady. The master artificer Hwui-Yin had fixed it up, but it was still a terrible instrument.

"Anyway, who does have the flower that my fan Kerry needs?"

The small band of English rebels hurried across the moonbow, frightened that they would be pursued by the mercenaries and trapped between the two Cornish forces. They had no idea of where they were going or what they would find, and no notion of where their next meal might come from.

Aelis was still carrying her bag of leaflets. A complete waste of time, and very cumbersome, but after inventing printing among fairies she did not intend to just dump them in the ocean.

In the theater Cal was directing his final late-night rehearsal. Despite a last minute scare when Titania had walked out again, things were now running smoothly. She had returned from a long sulk on the street outside bearing a beautiful flower, a present from the fairies she claimed, a story which pleased Cal as it showed she was getting into her part. Tomorrow was their first performance, and the day of the judging.

Theseus, Duke of Athens, and Hippolyta, his betrothed, swept onstage.

"Now, fair Hippolyta, our nuptial hour—," began Theseus.

"What the hell is this meant to be?" demanded Magenta, sweeping in through the open stage door. "Ancient Athenians didn't dress like that," she declared. "Looks nothing like an Athenian, and I should know. Who's this?"

"Hippolyta," said Cal, weakly.

"Hippolyta?" Magenta shrieked, placing her muscular self straight in front of the unfortunate actress. "Well, what's she doing here? Ancient Amazonian queens didn't get betrothed to Athenian nobles. Last thing they wanted to do. Completely ridiculous. Why don't you get back to your own tribe and get on with massacring the local males?"

Hippolyta wavered on the point of fleeing. The irate Magenta was a frightening sight.

The rest of the actors crowded out from backstage to see what was going on. Cal, desperate for his sensitive cast not to be upset on the eve of the opening, tried shooing Magenta away. She immediately gave him a muscular clout, batting him out of the way. His guitar thudded to the ground.

"Oh God, we're under attack," wailed Titania. "I knew I should never have got involved in this production. It's cursed."

"Don't leave," screamed Cal. "I need you."

"Well, I don't think you need her," said Heather, materializing brightly on Magenta's shoulder. "As a fairy queen she stinks."

"And what's this?" demanded Magenta, grabbing Titania by an imitation wing. "As I suspected. The triple-bloomed Welsh poppy." She wrenched it free.

Titania panicked and fled from the theater, along with a few minor characters.

Magenta grinned triumphantly.

"You soft Athenian dogs. No wonder Xenophon always preferred Spartans. And what's this?"

She picked up Cal's guitar and read the name on the neck.

"Gibson," she growled. "Stolen and no doubt from my good friend Johnny Thunders, you swine."

The English army formed up into ranks. A small group detached itself and advanced towards the opposition. The Chinese, Italians, Ghanaians and Irish numbered around six hundred altogether. The Cornish were in countless thousands.

"Surrender immediately," demanded the messengers, "and hand over Petal and Tulip. Otherwise we will cut you all to pieces."

"How dare you make war on us?" demanded Okailey, regally. "Have you forgotten how fairies are meant to behave?"

The appeal had no effect. Tala's army was rigidly disciplined and ruled by fear. No one dared disobey an order, no matter how much they wanted to.

Ailsa and Mairi stood on Kerry's fire escape and scanned the skies for a sign of the Scottish army, but the sky was empty.

"The Goddess knows where they've got to," grumbled Ailsa, and turned an accusing stare on Morag. "All you had to do was play one damn tune. You couldn't even do that without arguing."

Morag shrugged. It was too late now. After assaulting Heather with her fiddle she now had three broken strings. So had Heather, and they were both sporting bruises from vicious fiddle blows. After the fight Heather had disappeared somewhere to sulk.

"You have destroyed everything of value around you and caused general warfare on the streets. No doubt tomorrow you will find some spectacular new outrage to commit. On the Isle of Skye, you would have been drowned at birth."

"I have helped Kerry with her flower alphabet," replied Morag.

"With no success," countered Mairi. "If the MacLeod's had been involved the Welsh poppy would never have been lost."

Electronic wailing sounded from the next block.

"Why do sirens go off in this city all the time?"

"Good day's work, Heather."

Magenta trundled powerfully down Fourth Street.

"Caused chaos in Cal's play, regained the poppy for Kerry, and found Johnny Thunders' guitar.

But when they met Johnny it turned out not to be his guitar at all.

"Nice Gibson, he said, running his fingers up and down the fretboard. "But it's a recent model, not like mine. Look, Heather."

He showed the interested fairy exactly the way he played 'Born to Lose,' so she could show Kerry, which might help her make up with Morag. After a few more tunes, thin-sounding on the unamplified electric guitar, he played an oddly familiar air.

"How did you do that?" asked Heather as he finished a competent version of 'Tullochgorum.'

"I heard you play it enough times, sitting on top of the old theater."

A moonbow cut through the night to land at their feet.

"At last," said Agnes MacKintosh, Chief of the Clan, striding into view. "I thought we'd never find a familiar face. Well, Heather, what's happening?"

Kerry was out making one last determined effort to find a triple-bloomed Welsh poppy. Morag, in a huff with the MacLeod's, wandered out to the fire escape. She was surprised to find there Sheilagh MacPherson, Agnes MacKintosh and Jean MacLeod, mighty Clan Chiefs, climbing towards her, with Heather trailing sheepishly behind.

"We gave back the bits of the banner," said Morag immediately.

"And it was all an accident," added Heather.

"We have not come about the banner. We have come about the invasion."

"Although I would not mind a few words about the banner later," added Jean MacLeod.

Ailsa and Mairi gave their chief an enthusiastic welcome. Heather and Morag were not quite so enthusiastic about this turn of events. They still suspected that they were about to be dragged back to the Isle of Skye and thrown in a dungeon in Dunvegan Castle.

"The Scottish army was tricked into landing in the wrong place by a grim-tempered enemy of the fairies who played an evil version of 'Tullochgorum.'"

"That would be Dinnie."

"Well," said Sheilagh MacPherson. "We're here now, and no doubt Tala's army is as well. So let's not waste any time. The MacLeods have their banner and the MacKintoshes have their sword. Bring out the MacPherson Fiddle and we will go and scare them back across the ocean."

"Right,"said Morag. "The MacPherson Fiddle."

"The fiddle."

"The fiddle."

"Where is it?"

"The fiddle?"

"Yes, the fiddle!" exploded the MacPherson chief.

As it was last seen in several pieces in the gutter of East Fourth Street, this was a difficult question to answer.

Dinnie fell asleep in the park, not waking till it had got dark. He trudged home disgusted with life. Instead of making money busking he had wasted what little he had on beer, after which he had been in no condition to play properly. Furthermore, he had been harassed by an army of Scottish fairies and as Dinnie firmly believed that two Scots fairies had been one too many, a whole army made him feel that moving to New York had been a mistake.

"Well, they're not staying with me. I'll hang garlic and crucifixes in the windows. That'll keep them out."

Of course, Dinnie would not have a room to stay in before long. He could not pay the rent and was due to be evicted.

His misery intensified. He still craved Kerry. It had been a bad mistake to have sex with the woman from the health food shop, or at least a bad mistake to get caught.

On the theater steps he found Cal sitting with his head propped on his hands. Cal told him gloomily that his production of A Midsummer Night's Dream was ruined. Half his cast had fled, either scared by Magenta or panicked by Heather, and he did not even have a guitar to play the music. When the judges came the next day he would be laughed out of the competition.

"Kerry will win."

Dinnie thought this was probably a good thing but was too drunk and confused to think much about it and slouched upstairs to watch a little television before going to bed.

"Hi, I'm Linda. For the hottest two-girl phone sex in town, phone 970 F-U-C-K. We're waiting for your call."

THIRTY-EIGHT

After a brief lesson in the geography of New York from the MacLeod's the Scottish army marched over moonbows towards Central Park. There were many of them there, fairies from the MacKintoshes and their associates—the MacAndrews, the MacHardys, the MacPhails, the MacTavishes and others; the MacPhersons had brought the MacCurries, the MacGowans, the MacMurdochs, the MacClearys and more; the largest force of all was the huge grouping of the MacLeods and their numerous allies.

Right at the end marched Heather and Morag, in blackest disgrace. After the fate of the MacPherson Fiddle had been admitted, Sheilagh MacPherson had briskly informed the pair that if they thought they were in trouble before, it was nothing compared to the trouble they were in now. Once they got back to Scotland, incarceration in Dunvegan Castle would seem like a pleasant holiday compared to what she had in mind.

"Not that we will ever get back to Scotland, more than likely. Without the power of our three talismans we will be massacred here by Tala. Well done, Heather and Morag. Between yourselves you have managed to end several thousand years of Scottish fairy history."

Morag and Heather trudged unhappily over the roofs of the skyscrapers, muttering to each other that it was just not fair the way they were blamed for everything. They weren't to know that any of this would happen.

"What's more," whispered Morag, "I don't even want to be involved in any of this stuff. I'm not interested in clan warfare and feuds and stuff. I want to get on with our radical Celtic fairy punk band."

"Me too," agreed Heather. "Wait till I play you the Nuclear Assault album I stole from Dinnie."

Morag nudged her friend in the ribs.

"Look," she hissed. "There's that wee scunner Maggie MacGowan, showing off on the fiddle as usual."

They glowered at Maggie. She was entertaining the marchers with a slow and beautiful air, "The Flower o' the Quern."

"Boring bastard," muttered Morag. "If she tried that at the Thirteenth Street Squat she'd be bottled off the stage."

"And her version of 'Tullochgorum' is rubbish, I don't care what anyone says. And look! She's wearing shoes!"

The pair were aghast. Shoes were almost unheard of among fairies.

"The precious little tumshie."

The kilted hordes descended into Central Park, bagpipes skirling defiance. Ahead of them they could see the dark mass of Tala's army and nearby the small group of friendly defenders.

Everywhere claymores were unsheathed as the fairies made ready for their last hopeless battle. All around were grim-faced and serious. Morag and Heather decided to play a practical joke on the hated Wee Maggie MacGowan.

Johnny Thunders strummed a few tunes on Cal's Gibson, Magenta strode purposefully up Broadway and Dinnie could not sleep. He headed out to buy an egg-in-a-roll.

Kerry was sitting in the deli, sipping coffee.

She told him that her day had been a failure. There was not another triple-bloomed poppy to be found anywhere.

"Never mind. Enter your alphabet in the competition anyway. I happen to know that Cal's production of Shakespeare is heading for disaster, so you could still win."

Kerry explained that she could not possibly enter her alphabet unless it was complete.

"I'm pleased that Cal's play is a disaster, but he will win."

She sighed, and excused herself, saying that she was not feeling very well at all.

Dinnie munched his egg-in-a-roll, and ordered another. Kerry had not looked happy, but at least she hadn't mentioned the incident of the health food shop assistant.

THIRTY-NINE

"I'm not actually blaming you, Mairi MacLeod," said Jean, her Clan Chief, "but couldn't your second sight have warned us we were going to be outnumbered ten to one?"

Mairi shrugged hopelessly. Everyone else looked depressed. While some of the fairies were warlike most of them were not; and none of them, not even the fierce ones like Ailsa, had any idea of grand battle strategy.

"I'm reminded of Bannockburn," said Sheilagh MacPherson, referring to a famous battle where a small Scottish force defeated a much larger English one.

"Indeed," agreed Agnes MacKintosh. "A grand victory. Do you have any idea how it was achieved?"

"None at all. Of course, they had Robert the Bruce to lead them, which was a help. Personally I have never studied tactical warfare."

Neither had any of them. When it came right down to it, what the good Scottish fairies liked doing best was sitting with pleasant company in pleasant surroundings, playing music and drinking heather ale and whisky.

And this was fine, as until now that had seemed to be the main preoccupation of the English fairies as well. It would have been unthinkable for them to assemble such a huge host and go to war, before Tala took power.

"What is the matter with that King? He just does not act like a normal fairy."

"I blame the hole in the ozone layer," said Agnes. "I knew the humans would do for us eventually."

"Terrific," grumbled Maeve to Padraig. "These Scots arrive with grand tales of three mighty weapons to repel the English, and what happens? They mislay one of them. Ha!"

The park that evening had an evil atmosphere quite unlike the aura of peace the fairies had been spreading around previously, and while Tala's army was there, many crimes were committed in the area.

The Cornish army began to advance. The defenders braced themselves.

"Help is at hand," called a robust human voice. It was Magenta, marching in with a small fiddle in her hand.

"Freshly repaired by my good friend Hwui-Yin. You should have mentioned before that it was important to you."

It seemed like a miracle. The MacPherson Fiddle had arrived at the very last moment.

Sheilagh MacPherson touched the violin lovingly. In her mind she had a picture of its long history, and she knew now how it had come to be in America; MacPherson the Robber's heart-broken mermaid lover had borne it over the seas after he was hanged.

Jean MacLeod unfurled the banner. Agnes MacKintosh brandished the sword. Sheilagh MacPherson kissed the fiddle and handed it to Wee Maggie MacGowan.

"Right, Maggie. You are the finest fiddler in Scotland. Play 'Tullochgorum' and watch the enemy flee."

Maggie took the fiddle and stepped forward proudly in her red and black MacGowan kilt. Unfortunately Heather and Morag had tied her shoelaces together. She fell flat on her face and the fiddle smashed into pieces.

"If we can make it to Grand Central," whispered Heather, "we might get a train to Canada."

The ambulance took a long time to come through the busy traffic and when Kerry was loaded into it she was very ill. She was retching continually and though her stomach had emptied of food she was still bringing up some greenish liquid which dribbled down her chin on to her chest. Sweat dripped from her forehead and her face was deathly pale.

Eventually she reached St. Vincent's Hospital. When the doctor examined her he pronounced that the disease had spread from her large intestine to her small intestine and there was nothing to do but perform an ileostomy, which meant cutting it out. Kerry had begun to cry because she had been told in the past that if this happened it would be irreversible and she would always have to have a colostomy bag.

The doctor marked a cross on her right side with a thick blue felt-tipped pen where the surgeons were to cut, and the nurses made Kerry ready for the operation, giving her the first of her injections and strapping a little name-tag to here wrist. Kerry moaned and retched painfully as the poison from her ruptured intestines spread throughout her body. She brought up more greenish fluid which splashed horribly into the plastic bowl at her side.

Dinnie sat beside her in the ward. He had found Kerry in the street, too sick to open her front door. He called an ambulance and traveled with her to the hospital. Although the doctors had no time or inclination to give him information, he had learned about the disease from a more sympathetic nurse. Seeing Kerry looking like death he felt very sorry indeed.

FORTY

There was no need to ask who had tied Maggie MacGowan's shoelaces together. Before Agnes MacKintosh could actually run the culprits through with her sword, Magenta intervened.

"Excuse me, fellow warrior chiefs," she said, "but are you all just going to stand here in a bundle waiting to be attacked?"

"What else is there to do?"

"Form squares, of course. Have you no idea of tactics? I have just led an army through hostile territory against vastly superior forces. Of course, my troops are experienced Hoplites and Pelasts and you are small fairies, but perhaps we can save the day anyway."

This was obviously a woman who knew what she was talking about. The defenders were quickly organized into two hollow squares. Given time, Magenta would have issued precise instructions for the central squares to withdraw in good order when attacked, thereby drawing the enemy in and trapping them in pincer movement with her flanking forces (much as Hannibal had done at Cannae), but she knew the fairies would not be able to do this sort of thing at short notice.

When the Cornish army attacked with an ear-shattering roar, the plan seemed to work. Despite large disparity of forces, the squares held. The Italians, Chinese, Ghanaians, Scots and Irish all stood firm, jabbing with their swords, and the undisciplined attacking horde was unable to break through.

High up in the sky Aelric and his rebels looked down at the scene.

"The Goddess damn that Tala," exploded Aelric. "Now he's trying to massacre these poor fairies as well."

Aelis did not reply. She had noticed that for the first time the Cornish had no scouts flying high in defense.

Up at dawn, Cal checked his scenery, some of which had been damaged during Magenta's last assault on the theater. What was left of his cast would arrive during the morning, as the performance had to be judged at noon.

Cal dreaded to think what it would be like. His carefully rehearsed play was now full of emergency understudies, some of whom had never even read the script. He himself was playing the part of Lysander after the actor had said he would not work in a building where fairies jabbed at him with little claymores.

Outside on the steps sat Joshua, drowsy but unable to sleep properly. Without his cocktail his body did not feel right. He swore that he would kill Magenta if he did not die first.

FORTY-ONE

Dinnie sat in the hospital restaurant. It was not a pleasant experience. He hated being surrounded by sick people, particularly old hopeless sick people with dressing gowns and bored-looking relatives.

Every so often he would take the lift to Kerry's ward and enquire after her, but the operation was a long one and the nurses had no information. After this Dinnie would go back to the restaurant, each time feeling that he should have done something more, like demanding loudly that the nurses stop keeping the truth from him and tell him everything they knew. Unfortunately the nurses seemed rather intimidating close up. Presumably they developed their muscles hauling patients in and out of bed. Dinnie remained polite, but fretful.

Time never goes so slowly as when waiting in a hospital and after a few hours Dinnie felt as blank as the hopeless cases in dressing gowns.

"We have held them off once, but I do not think we can do so again."

Jean MacLeod, as dark-haired, beautiful and dangerous as

the MacLeod sisters only even taller and fiercer, held the newly repaired green banner high in defiance and prepared to try.

"To hell with this," muttered Morag, somewhere in the middle of a defensive square. "Could we not sneak away somewhere?"

Heather was in full agreement but surrounded on all sides as they were, it was impossible.

"We'll just have to stay here and be massacred."

"I don't want to be massacred. I want to have fun in the city. I like this city. I like all the pizzas and delis and shops open all the time and gigs and nightclubs and bright clothes and bright people and huge buildings. In fact, apart from the poor people dying on the streets, I like everything about it. I am even getting used to the funny sweet whisky."

"Me too," agreed Heather. "Although it is not a patch on the braw malt the MacKintoshes brew. We could have fun here if all these fools would just behave peacefully for a change. Did Kerry finish making me my Red Indian headband?"

"Yes, and it will look very very fine indeed, if you ever get a chance to wear it. What's that?"

Tala's army was readying itself for its second attack when, from far above on the visible moonbow, more fairy figures appeared.

"Do you really think this will work?" asked Aelric, emptying out handfuls of propaganda leaflets.

"It might," replied Aelis, flying beside him. "I have a talent for propaganda, though I say it myself."

"WORKERS FREE YOURSELVES," read the leaflets, spinning down from the sky in their thousands.

Kerry was being wheeled back into a quiet ward after her operation. The nurses informed Dinnie that it had not been necessary to remove her small intestine after all. Once she had been opened up the damage had turned out not to be as serious as was thought. This was something that could happen with Crohn's disease, attacks appearing worse than they actually were. So Kerry still had some hope of the reversal operation.

"But what a terrible trauma," said Dinnie. "I feel awful."

"It's worse for her," said the nurse.

"Will she be better now?"

Apparently not. She might have another serious attack tomorrow, or in ten minutes' time.

FORTY-TWO

Dinnie caught a cab back to Fourth Street to pick up some belongings for Kerry. Being concerned about her, he did not resent the fare. Love can change anything. He let himself in with her key, packed a bag and called over to the theater just as Cal's play was getting under way. Without pausing to watch, he hurried on upstairs.

Cal's play was exactly the disaster he had expected it to be. The unrehearsed replacements forgot their lines, the emergency tape of background music kept blaring out in mid-scene and the remaining original actors crept nervously around the stage, expecting at any moment to be attacked by bag ladies or fairies.

The small audience giggled and the three judges, all local artists, writhed with embarrassment.

"I knew the standard would be low," they whispered to each other, "but this is a disgrace."

Upstairs Dinnie washed and changed quickly. He yawned. He had to return to the hospital but a wave of tiredness threatened to overcome him. Spying his fiddle on the bed, he had an urge to revive himself with a quick tune.

He picked it up and let go with a strong version of 'Tullochgorum.'

Immediately a moonbow sprang into the theater downstairs and screaming fairies poured in from all directions.

These were the last skirmishes of the battle in Central Park, a battle which had turned out to be not so fierce after all. The propaganda leaflets, prepared by Aelis with all the skills of a born marketing genius, had roused deep, hidden feelings in the ranks of the English army. Denied access to outside information for so long, the strong and simple arguments in the leaflets went straight to their hearts.

"Why *do* we work for twelve hours a day for little wages? We used to be free to do anything we wanted."

"Why *do* we have to worship this horrible new god? I liked our old Goddess."

"Why *do* we let Tala and a few thugs rule over us?"

"And what are we doing here, fighting other fairies?"

The ranks of the army began to break up as the fairies, roused from a nightmare, realized the stupidity of their situation. Foot soldiers everywhere refused to advance as ordered. The barons, themselves dubious of Tala's power, felt their authority over their serfs start to crumble.

The situation, however, was far from resolved. Tala's large group of mercenaries showed no inclination to change sides. Nor did the Royal Guard, led by Marion his stepdaughter. Things could still have been disastrous had not Aelric, floating down on the breeze, suddenly spied the triple-bloomed Welsh poppy in Magenta's shopping bag and snatched it up.

"Change sides, lovely Marion," he said. "Join the peasants' revolt and this rare triple-bloomed Welsh poppy in red, orange and yellow, will be yours. Your alphabet will be complete."

Marion looked at the poppy, quickly scanned a propaganda leaflet, and changed sides, taking the Royal Guard with her. The battle was over and New York was safe.

The only ones not to give in were the mercenaries. Seeing that all was lost but unwilling to surrender, they magicked a moonbow to escape.

"You have to admire them," said Magenta, as they sped away. "They are good mercenaries."

Dinnie, hurrying downstairs, was surprised to hear such a commotion from the theater. Presuming that the audience were throwing things at the stage, he could not resist a quick look.

Inside there was chaos. Although Dinnie could not know it, his rendering of 'Tullochgorum' had attracted the moonbow, and the mercenaries had barged into the performance followed by a fierce assortment of pursuers.

Confused by the battle in this strange city, and never having seen *A Midsummer Night's Dream* before, the mercenaries were horrified to find themselves surrounded by gigantic fairies. Assuming that these on-stage extras wandering round in cardboard wings were in fact part of the enemy, the mercenaries materialized to fight them, which forced their pursuers to do the same.

Actors fled in panic as fairies of all colors fought and flew round the stage. Cal screamed for everyone to leave him alone. The judges gaped in wonder in the back row.

Dinnie noticed the three judges, and thought briefly that one of them looked familiar, but his attention was diverted by Heather pounding down on to his shoulder.

"Hello, Dinnie," she screamed in his ear. "Just mopping-up operations. Nothing to worry about."

She gave him a brief explanation of what had happened but Dinnie paid little attention.

"You dumb fairies," he shouted. "Kerry is sick in the hospital. I'm going there now."

He left, not caring either way about their stupid fighting. He was pleased, though, that Cal's play had been such a spectacular disaster.

FORTY-THREE

With the battle over the fairies partied on the East Village rooftops. Heather and Morag were absent. As soon as they could they had rushed off to visit Kerry in the hospital.

They told her the events of the momentous day, and arranged flowers in her hair.

Kerry propped herself up on her elbows.

"Touch my fingers," she said. "I need some strength."

The MacLeod sisters had got good and drunk along with everyone else during the afternoon, but as friends of Kerry they had some interest in the competition and floated down to eavesdrop on the judges.

They were surprised to learn that they knew one of the judges. It was Joshua, recruited from the streets as part of the "Art in the Community Program."

"They will be saying what a grim disaster Cal's play was," said Ailsa, with certainty. "It's an awful shame that Kerry could not enter her alphabet."

A cab drew up outside the theater. A skeletal-looking Kerry emerged in a blue dressing gown and yellow fringed waistcoat. Dinnie helped her up the steps.

Much too ill to have left her hospital bed, Kerry had come for her flower.

"Where is Aelric?" she demanded. Seónaid MacLeod flew

up to the roof and reappeared with Aelric, who held Marion's hand. Marion had the flower wrapped around her beaded black hair.

"Give," said Kerry, holding out her hand. Marion unwrapped the flower and handed it over.

Kerry's face was radiant with pleasure. She handed the bloom to Dinnie.

"Enter my alphabet in the competition," she instructed. The fairies clapped and cheered at this act of heroism by someone so gravely ill.

Kerry collapsed on to the ground. She was taken back to the hospital and Dinnie notified the judges that the Ancient Celtic Flower Alphabet was now ready for inspection.

Magenta marched triumphantly into East Fourth Street. Her mighty generalship had won another stupendous victory and she had come to join in the celebrations.

Everywhere in the street fairies were drinking, partying and fucking; and it was in the aftermath of this gathering that the first mixed-race fairies were born.

The MacLeod's, confidently expecting triumph for Kerry's flower alphabet, were dismayed by an unexpected turn of events. They learned that *A Midsummer Night's Dream* had not gone down so badly after all.

"The most amazing on-stage effects we have ever seen," said the judges.

"Quite staggering the way the piece evoked the world of fairies. I could have sworn they were really there. Of course, some of it was rather ragged but I have to admit I was very impressed."

"The flower alphabet is a beautiful and unique piece of Celtic folklore . . . but does it compare to such a vibrant rendition of Shakespeare?"

"Oh no," groaned Rhona. "Kerry must not lose after half killing herself to come from the hospital. And feeding us all these oatcakes."

Heather and Morag appeared back from the hospital. They all had an emergency meeting in the deli, but no solution presented itself.

"We could bribe the judges."

"With what?"

"We'll rob a bank."

This idea was quickly vetoed.

Sheilagh MacPherson sought Magenta out to thank her for returning the fiddle and helping them in the battle, proclaiming her a friend of the MacPhersons for life. The intoxicated Chief of the Clan clapped Magenta heartily on the back and told her about the latest progress in the judging.

"What a determined young woman that Kerry is," said Magenta admiringly. "I will have her in my army any time."

"Well she won't be winning this competition if she is a friend of yours," pronounced Joshua, appearing beside her. "Because I am a judge. And after I have awarded the prize to Cal I am going to come and beat you to death."

FORTY-FOUR

"The young woman is undecided, but the young man liked Cal's play best," announced Morag, back from spying on the judges.

"And Joshua will pick Cal," wailed Heather. "He'll win."

They sat in the theater on top of a fake pillar, part of the Athenian court. Dinnie slouched nearby. Sheilagh MacPherson and Agnes MacKintosh fluttered up unsteadily.

"We know of your problem," they said. "And we are sympathetic because we understand that Kerry has been a good friend to stray fairies and this man Cal has treated her badly. We do not like boyfriends who act badly. We will help with part of the problem."

"How?"

"Are you familiar with *A Midsummer Night's Dream* ?"

They were, a little.

"Then you will know," said Agnes, "that it involves a magic herb which, once spread on the eyes, makes the person fall in love with the first person he sees. Dinnie, fellow MacKintosh, bring me the herb."

Dinnie, momentarily hopeful, shook his head sadly. The Chief of the Clan was even more stupid than the rest of them. She apparently did not know the difference between a stage prop and real life.

"It's only a weed from the sidewalk," he said.

"To you, maybe. To mighty chiefs of Scottish fairy clans, not necessarily. Bring it here."

Dinnie found and brought the weed. Agnes and Sheilagh flew shakily across to Joshua and touched it to his eyes. They propelled him with a few gentle sword jabs towards Magenta.

He screwed up his eyes and opened them.

"Magenta. I have always loved you."

"Then vote for Kerry in the competition."

"Of course."

"Have some Fitzroy cocktail," said Magenta, slipping her hand into his. "I will share the recipe with you."

There was now one vote each. The young woman, a local sculptor, was still pondering.

"I can tell she liked the play the best," sighed the psychic Mairi.

"You stupid fairies," muttered Dinnie as they passed him in the hospital waiting room. "All the excitement you caused made Kerry ill."

"Nonsense," replied Heather. "Crohn's disease strikes down many people who have never seen a fairy. However, as you are now being nice to Kerry, I may yet rob a bank to pay your rent. We're going to visit her now."

"It isn't visiting time yet."

"An important difference between fairies and humans is that we are small and invisible and you are not. We don't have to wait for visiting time."

Dinnie glowered at them. Beside him in the waiting room were two other young men to see Kerry and he was jealous.

Inside, Kerry was weak but pleased to see the fairies. Morag hopped onto the bed.

"You won the prize."

Kerry let out a small whoop of delight.

"Dinnie did it in the end," announced Heather, proud of her fellow MacKintosh. "At the vital moment he walked up to the last judge, introduced himself politely and asked her if, as well as being a local sculptor, she could possibly be the well-known Linda, star of the hottest two-girl phone sex in town. She was thrilled to be recognized, particularly when Dinnie said what a great fan of hers he was and asked for her autograph. After that she was putty in his hands and voted for you.

"The Community Arts Prize is now yours, and well deserved. Cal will regret not teaching you the guitar break from 'Bad Girl' for the rest of his life."

Morag muscled her way back into the conversation.

"There are hordes of men outside waiting for dates with you," she said. "I would recommend playing the field for a while. In the meantime, let me introduce my friends."

She gestured to a group of fairies behind her, each of whom greeted Kerry politely.

"This is Sheilagh MacPherson and this is Agnes MacKintosh and this is Jean MacLeod. They are our Clan Chiefs and as such have great powers of healing. With them is Flora MacGillvray, a healer renowned throughout Scotland.

"This is Donal, a friend of Maeve's. He is the healer of the O'Brien tribe and famous in Ireland for his skill. This is Cheng Tin-Hung, healer of the Chinese, Lucretia, healer from the Italians, and Aba, healer from the Ghanaians. All of them possess great skill and great reputations.

"It is the finest collection of fairy physicians ever assembled. Do not mind the powerful aroma of whisky. Even intoxication does not lessen the powers of a fairy healer.

"We would like to point out that things are not as bad as you think, because you are talented, popular, pleasant and beautiful, and that being the case, so what if you have a colostomy bag, you are still streets ahead of most humans. But we will spare you the lecture and let the healers get on with their work."

"And if eight powerful fairies can't fix your insides," said Heather, "we will be most surprised. Morag and I will now withdraw and organize your homecoming party, and say goodbye to the English. They are hurrying home to tear down the workhouses and resume pleasurable lives getting drunk under bushes. Magenta has wandered off happily with Joshua, pleased because she thinks he voted for her as head of the Greek army. Callum MacHardie is fixing the MacPherson Fiddle. Our Clan Chiefs have forgiven us our few misdemeanors because everything has turned out well in the end."

"That is news to us," said their Clan Chiefs.

"Well, haven't you?"

The Chiefs said they would think about it, and Morag and Heather exited while they were ahead.

"What's happening?" demanded Dinnie, outside.

"Powerful fairy magic," replied Heather. "And you may come to Kerry's welcome-home party providing you bring a suitably expensive present. I believe she has her eye on a set of silver bangles from an Indian shop. You may yet end up going out with her if you take a sound line on which flowers are best in her hair, pretend to like Botticelli and bring good presents.

"Meanwhile we are off for a few drams and a bit of serious fiddling. If the Irish and everyone else think they've heard Scottish music at its best just because Wee Maggie MacGowan managed to struggle through a few simple tunes without making any mistakes, they have a lot to learn.

"Collum MacHardie has promised to make us some amplifiers. When our radical Celtic band gets going, the hills and glens will never be the same."

Johnny Thunders left Cal's Gibson in the theater. It was a good guitar but he could not bring himself to keep it. He knew how bad it felt to have your guitar stolen.

It was time for him to be off, though his mission had been a failure. Thinking that before he left he might as well take one last look around, he headed for Kerry's. He had a desire to see the flower alphabet that had caused so much excitement.

Inside, he was impressed. The flowers, dried by Kerry and spoken to kindly by Morag, emanated great beauty and power. The thirty-three blooms were laid out on the floor and behind them as background Kerry had arranged all her favorite things, including her New York Dolls bootlegs and her remixed copy of the Heartbreakers album.

Another of her favorite things was her guitar.

"My 1958 Gibson Tiger Top."

Johnny picked it up.

"She had it all the time. No wonder she is obsessed with the New York Dolls."

Whichever lover had given Kerry the guitar must have been the person who stole it all those years ago.

He made to leave with it but stopped, staring again at the beautiful flowers. He thought about Kerry lying sick in the hospital.

"Oh, to hell with it. I'll take the old beat-up thing I got from that bag lady. I always could play better than anyone else on any old guitar."

He left Kerry's guitar where it lay, and was not dissatisfied.